Karyn and her husband Roy had come to the peaceful California village of Drago to escape the savagery of the city.

On the surface Drago appeared to be like most small rural towns.

But it was not.

The village had a most unsavory history.

Unexplained disappearances, sudden deaths.

People just vanished, never to be found.

Fawcett Gold Medal Books
by Gary Brandner:

☐ HELLBORN 14414 $2.50

☐ THE HOWLING 13824 $2.50

☐ THE HOWLING II 14091 $2.50

☐ WALKERS 14319 $2.50

Gary Brandner

THE HOWLING

FAWCETT GOLD MEDAL • NEW YORK

THE HOWLING

© 1977 GARY BRANDNER

Published by Fawcett Gold Medal Books,
a unit of CBS Publications, the Consumer Publishing Division
of CBS Inc.

ISBN 0-449-13824-0

Printed in the United States of America

12   11   10

THE
HOWLING

In the dark Arda Forest on the border between Greece and Bulgaria there is a dead gray patch of land roughly one mile square where no one goes and nothing lives. Today no map marks the location; no road leads there. Four hundred years ago it was a village. It was called Dradja.

Even when the village lived it was a place of darkness. Peasants from the surrounding lands made the sign of the cross when they spoke its name. They entered only when they had to, and left as soon as their business was done. Passing travelers were warned to avoid the place. Some who did not heed the warning would later wish they had.

The stories told about Dradja were unfocused and often conflicting. On one point they all agreed: there was Evil in the village. The Evil took various forms, depending on the storyteller. Travelers listened to the stories and nodded. It was bad, but it was not their concern. They would skirt the village and cross themselves and tell each other that some things were best left alone. In the bleak autumn of 1583, all this changed.

In that season a shepherd named Kyust, with his wife

Anya and his little daughter, brought his flock to the rich fields near Dradja. The land to the north, where Kyust had always grazed his sheep, had suffered through a terrible drought, and moving the flock was the only way to keep the animals from starving. Kyust had heard the dark tales of Dradja, but his need was greater than his fear.

At sundown of his first day Kyust settled his sheep and then returned to his cottage. After a family supper, he fell into a deep sleep. In the morning he found three of his young lambs savagely killed, and the mother ewe bleating pathetically over the remains. The shepherd brought in a dog to keep watch through the next night. In the morning it, too, was dead.

Kyust knew the family could not survive without his flock. He had to catch the killer of his sheep. Through the next night he stayed with his flock in the fields. So that his wife would not be alone with their daughter, he sent for his sister Rachel.

Kyust spent a quiet, uneventful night and then worked all the following day. That evening, his little daughter, who had been playing in a nearby meadow, did not return home. Anya and Rachel called to her and searched as far from the cottage as they dared. Finally, Rachel ran to the field to get Kyust, and all three began to search. In a grove of alder trees near a stream where the child often played, Anya found what remained of her daughter. The small body was so badly torn it was barely recognizable as human.

When the shepherd saw what had been done to his child he let out one horrible scream. He swore vengeance and set off for the village of Dradja, vowing to destroy the Evil that lived there, whatever form it took.

The shepherd Kyust never returned. The sheep, untended, wandered away. Rachel stayed by the side of her sister, who refused to leave without her husband. Knowing she must have help, Rachel left the cottage one morning and journeyed many hours to a place where Gypsies often made their camp. To one of the Gypsies she gave a message for her brothers in their home village, telling of the tragedies that had befallen Anya, and asking the brothers to come for them.

In her haste to return to the cottage Rachel chose a shortcut that took her close to Dradja. Night had fallen by the time she passed the village, and a flurry of movement caught her attention. What she saw in Dradja was horrible beyond belief. The black secret of the place was the last thing she would ever experience.

When her brothers, having received her message, found her mangled body, they gathered a hundred men from their village and marched on Dradja. Armed with clubs, axes, pikes, and a few matchlock firearms, they swarmed into the accursed village and herded the people into the center of town. They ordered the guilty to step forward. No one moved.

It was clear then what had to be done. In that bloody day every man, woman, and child caught in Dradja was tortured to death. When the ground of the village was a crimson swamp the bodies were stacked with layers of dry wood, soaked with pitch, and set afire. The animals were slaughtered, the village itself put to the torch. When nothing remained of Dradja but ashes, these were plowed under. The fresh-turned earth was sown and sown again, but not even a weed would grow.

CHAPTER ONE

~~~~~~

The September heat lay heavy on Los Angeles. In the condominium community called Hermosa Terrace all the windows were tightly closed. The only sounds were the hum of exhaust fans and the muted growl of a power mower.

In the living room of Unit Two, Karyn Beatty stood on tiptoe to kiss her husband, Roy. Lady, their miniature collie, wagged her approval from the sofa. It started as a casual husband-and-wife first-anniversary kiss, but it quickly became something more. Karyn drew back her head and looked into Roy's clear brown eyes.

"Are you trying to start something?" she said a little breathlessly.

"Darn right," Roy replied, taking her in his arms.

Roy pulled her close, his big, gentle hands warm through the thin material of her summer dress. He kissed her neck where the blond hair curled forward below her ear.

"Won't Chris be here soon?" she said, her lips close to his ear.

"We won't answer the door."

"You couldn't do that to your best friend. Especially after we asked him to come by for an anniversary drink."

"I suppose you're right," Roy admitted. "Anyway, he won't stay long. He has a date."

"Anybody we know?"

"A new one, I think."

"Doesn't Chris ever get serious about anybody?"

"Who knows? I think he's secretly in love with you."

"You don't mean it?"

"Why not? All my friends have good taste."

Max Quist shut off the power mower and took out a soiled handkerchief to wipe the sweat from his face. He watched as a young couple in sparkling tennis whites climbed out of a sports car and ran laughing across the lawn. They didn't pay any attention to Max. Nobody living in Hermosa Terrace paid any attention to Max. He was like another piece of shrubbery to them. No, he thought, not even that much. Max hated these people. He hated them for having all the things he would never have. He would quit this lousy job in a minute if it weren't for his parole officer. Just once he would like to show the smug sonsofbitches that Max Quist was *somebody*.

The telephone rang in Unit Two. Roy Beatty picked it up and frowned as he listened to the voice on the other end. He spoke briefly and hung up.

"Anything wrong?" Karyn asked.

"I've got to go to Anaheim. Deliver some books."

"On Saturday? On our anniversary?"

"Dammit, it's my own fault. I promised to drop off a set of inspection manuals at Aerodyne yesterday. Had them in the trunk of the car and forgot all about it. I don't know how it slipped my mind."

Karyn smiled. It *was* very unlike Roy to forget anything. He was always thoroughly organized, like one of the technical manuals he edited. When she had first met him she had thought Roy Beatty was as stodgy as a church deacon. However, she had soon discovered his warm sense of humor, an open-minded willingness to listen, and a depth of intellect that was not apparent in his All-American good looks. Karyn had been working as a convention hostess for the New York Hilton at the time. Roy was in the city for a gathering of engineers. For the first time, she had broken the hotel rule against socializing with the guests. Roy had stayed on for a week after the convention, and they had been together constantly. When he had returned to the Coast he had said he would be back for her on his vacation. She had not expected him to come, but he had. That was when she had finally admitted she loved him.

"Don't be long," she said as he stood at the door. She kissed him and watched him walk down the winding path through the neatly trimmed shrubbery. Karyn could not imagine how she could be happier. She had Roy and she had an excellent job with a hotel near the airport where she was in line for convention manager when her current boss retired. Tonight she would give Roy her special anniversary gift—the news that he was going to be a father. Yes, her life was just about perfect.

Max Quist watched the blond young man come out of Unit Two and stride down the walk past him without a flicker. Max might as well have been invisible. The woman stood in the doorway watching him go. Good-looking cunt. Too good-looking. Both of them. Like people in a magazine ad. Young, beautiful, healthy, rich. Max spat on the cropped grass. How he wanted to show them what it's like to be hurt. Hurt them. Yes . . . hurt them.

Karyn was in the kitchen putting the lunch things away when the doorbell chimed. Chris was early, she thought. She dried her hands and walked out through the living room to the door. She did not bother to look through the tiny viewer. She never did. There was no danger here. This was Hermosa Terrace, not East Los Angeles.

Karyn opened the door and the heat pushed against the cool inside air. The man in the doorway was not Chris Halloran. He smiled at her.

"Yes?" Karyn said when the man did not speak right away.

He had thick black hair that was poorly barbered. His cotton workshirt was dark with perspiration under the arms. He seemed vaguely familiar.

"I'm supposed to check the pipes in your bathroom," he said.

"There's nothing wrong with our pipes."

"It's in the apartment next door. Their shower don't drain right, and it might be plugged up where your drain pipes come together."

Something in the way the man spoke was wrong. The short speech sounded rehearsed. Something about the man himself was wrong. He continued to smile.

"You'd better come back when my husband is here. He knows about those things."

Without making any sudden moves the man had somehow come through the doorway and was standing in the living room. He was still smiling, but it was a different smile. "That's okay," he said. "We won't need your husband."

Over on the couch Lady raised her neat little head and pricked her ears at the strange male voice. After a moment she put her head back down on her paws, but remained watchful.

"I'm sorry, but I'd rather you didn't come in now." Karyn fought to still the tremor of fear in her voice.

"But I *am* in," the man said. He reached behind him and closed the door. Without taking his eyes off Karyn he turned the small knob, shooting the dead-bolt lock into place.

"What do you think you're doing?" Karyn wanted her voice to be angry and strong, but the fear was in her now. She could not hide it.

"You know what I'm doing," the man said.

"I—I don't keep much money in the house. You can have what there is. And my jewelry."

"I don't want your money or your jewelry. But you know that, don't you? You know what I want, and you're going to give it to me." He reached out suddenly and squeezed her breast.

Karyn jumped back as though from an electric shock.

"Please, leave me alone!" The sour smell of his body was sharp in her nostrils. "M-my husband will be home."

"No he won't. He just left. We have all the time we need."

She took a careful step backward. The man's eyes traveled over her body, probing at her. His hands shot out and seized her wrists.

"No!" she cried.

"Relax," he said. "You're going to like it."

"Please . . . you can't . . ."

The man pulled Karyn against his body and mashed his mouth down on hers. Karyn clamped her jaws together as his tongue pushed in past her lips. He tasted of stale cigarettes.

"Where's the bedroom?"

Karyn shook her head from side to side, afraid to trust her voice.

With a sudden movement the man twisted one arm up behind her back, forcing her to walk in front of him. He marched Karyn into the hallway that opened between the living room and the room Roy used for a den. She stumbled along in his grasp past the bathroom to the open door, through which they could see the bed.

All the things she had read about rape tumbled through Karyn's mind. All the advice for women. Fight back. Don't fight back. Scream. Stay calm. Blow a whistle. Run. Reason with the man.

Lovely advice, all useless. Fight the man? He was at least seventy pounds heavier than she, and certainly stronger. Scream? Who would hear? Hermosa Terrace Townhomes were proud of their soundproofing. Reason with him? Reason with an animal?

They were in the bedroom now. The man spun Karyn around and pushed her backward onto the bed.

The thinking part of her mind shut off and instinct took over. She crossed her arms protectively over her breasts and drew back her feet to kick out at the man when he came at her.

The man laughed at her efforts and batted the kick aside with an easy swipe of his hand. He grasped her by the ankles and forced her legs apart. Karyn writhed on the bed, helpless against his strength.

The man grinned down at her, showing large, strong teeth. Droplets of sweat stood out on his forehead and upper lip. His eyes moved down to her crotch. Karyn felt open and exposed with the thin velour pants pulled tight between her legs.

"I'm pregnant," she said suddenly.

"Bullshit."

"I *am*," she insisted. "Three months."

"Then you don't have to worry about getting knocked up, do you?"

He released one of Karyn's ankles and took hold of the velour pants at the waist. He yanked them down, exposing the smooth, pale skin of her belly. The snap and zipper held at first, but he tugged again and the material tore away.

Then she screamed. Not with any thought of summoning help or frightening the man off. A visceral scream of outrage and terror.

"Shut up!" he ordered. He leaned forward and slapped her hard on the face. She stopped screaming.

A sudden high-pitched barking behind the man spun him around. Lady stood braced on her little legs, yapping angrily. The man swung his foot in a vicious arc; the toe of his heavy shoe caught the little dog just below the ribs and lifted her off the floor.

Lady yelped in surprise and pain. Never before had anyone deliberately hurt her. She crouched on the floor whimpering, her eyes pleading for an apology, a comforting pat.

"Get out of here, mutt," the man snapped.

Still whimpering, Lady moved uncertainly toward the door. She stopped and looked back toward her mistress. The man made a threatening motion with his hand, and the dog retreated into the hall. The man kicked the door shut behind her.

"Hell of a watchdog you've got there." He grinned and came at Karyn again.

"Please don't do this. Please don't hurt me." Even as the words came out, Karyn knew they were useless. This unspeakable thing was actually going to happen to her. *Was* happening to her. What had she ever done that she should be brutalized this way?

The man was upon her again, and Karyn's mind ceased to function logically. He tore away the nylon bikini pants, and his fingers crawled over and into her.

Abruptly he dropped to his knees and thrust his face up between her legs. He clamped his mouth on her, and Karyn could feel his tongue like a thick, wet worm probing, probing at her. She pummeled his head with her fists, but the blows had no effect.

Then he pulled his face back and bit her high on the soft inside of the thigh. He bit down hard, and his teeth sank into the clean white flesh until the blood flowed. Karyn's back arched up off the bed in reaction to the pain.

When the man at last unclenched his jaw and stood over her again his lips were crimson with her blood. Breathing in short, harsh bursts, he reached down and unzipped the front of his pants. Karyn twisted her head away, but could not shut out the sight as he freed himself from the damp jockey shorts and bore down on her.

He forced her legs farther apart and positioned himself between them. Blood from the throbbing bite wound left a red smear on the bedspread. With one cruel thrust he invaded her body.

Karyn cried out in pain and rage. She scrabbled at his face with both hands, clawing for his eyes.

"Bitch!" He hit her in the face with a rock-hard fist.

Karyn tasted blood, and the room swam for a moment, but she continued to use her nails to slash at the face above her.

The man pulled out of her for a moment and drove a fist into her bare belly. Karyn felt something break inside, and there was no fight left in her.

"That's better." He planted his hands on her shoulders and rammed into her again.

Karyn squeezed her eyes shut. When she was a little girl in the dentist chair and the drill hurt her, she would dig her nails into her palms, making a small hurt to ease the larger one. She did it now. The lower part of her body was on fire. The wound on her thigh screamed. The man continued to pump away at her, grunting with every thrust.

Get it over with! she cried inside her head. *Get it over with and go away or kill me or whatever you're going to do. Just finish!*

And at last he did.

After endless minutes he withdrew and wiped himself with the satin bedspread. Karyn rolled her head on the pillow and looked up at him, but now the man would not meet her eye. Hurriedly he zipped up his pants and went out into the hall. Karyn heard him go through the living room.

She sat up on the bed and winced at the tearing pain in her stomach. Her insides felt loose, as though they might slide out between her legs when she stood up. She pulled the remains of the velour pants up over the mess on her lower belly and walked carefully to the door. She made it as far as the bathroom and vomited into the toilet.

She knelt there for several minutes on the cold tile with her hands gripping the sides of the bowl, waiting for the spasms of her stomach to ease. The sudden sound of someone moving around in the living room brought back the fear. When the bedroom door opened and the heavy footsteps came toward her she started to scream.

CHAPTER
TWO

~~~~~~

When Chris Halloran found Karyn on her knees in the bathroom she was sobbing incoherently. Finding the front door open, he had sensed something was wrong. He walked in, and that was when Karyn began to scream. Chris held her in his arms for five minutes before she could tell him what had happened. He called the police, then left a message for Roy at the Aerodyne Company in Anaheim.

The two months that followed were a painful time for Karyn. The blow she had taken to the stomach had brought on a miscarriage, but no permanent damage. There was an infection from the bite wound on her thigh that was slow to respond to medication. The doctor advised against plastic surgery until the scar had completely healed.

The police, using their new, more sympathetic procedures for rape victims, made that part of Karyn's ordeal as easy as they could. Her description of the rapist led them at once to Max Quist, the handyman, who had a record of assaults on women. Confronted with Karyn's positive identification, Quist pleaded guilty.

It was psychologically that Karyn suffered most. Twice-weekly sessions with an analyst helped a little, and group sessions brought her together with other women who had been raped. Still, her recovery was painfully slow. She would wake up in the night, eyes wide and staring, and scream that someone was biting her. Of all the violations of her body, it was the horror of the teeth sinking into her flesh that she could not erase. She returned to work, but her life at home with Roy suffered. She could not feel comfortable in their love-making.

The analyst suggested to Karyn and Roy that they go away from Los Angeles for a while. Restful, rural surroundings, he said, would be the best thing for Karyn's full recovery. The people at Karyn's hotel were understanding, giving her a six-month leave of absence. Roy worked out an arrangement with his firm, and they began taking trips out of the city to look for a place.

A friend in the real-estate business told them about an available house in a town to the north called Drago. They drove up to see it, but Karyn was not enthusiastic. The house was weathered and weed-grown, a mile outside the town, which Karyn thought looked like a cheerless cluster of wooden buildings. Roy, however, took to the place immediately. He assured Karyn that the house could be fixed up so she would love it. With some misgivings, she acquiesced.

For the next couple of weeks Roy made the trip alone to see that work on the house was being done to his specifications. He did not want Karyn to see it, he said. She would be surprised. When it was time to move in, he left a day early to see to last-minute details. Chris Halloran volunteered to drive Karyn up to the house.

It was a crisp November day when Chris headed north on Interstate 5 with Karyn beside him in the Camaro. In the back Lady stood with her front paws braced on the seat and her face thrust into the wind from the open window.

They left the freeway for a two-lane blacktop road that snaked up into the Tehachapi Mountains. The outside air grew chill as they climbed.

"Do you want me to roll up the window?" Chris asked.

Karyn moved her head, letting the wind play with her loose blond hair. "No, it feels good. Clean."

As they drove on the evergreen forest pushed in closer on both sides of the road.

"How much farther is the town?" said Chris.

"A few miles. Just over the ridge up ahead and down into the valley. Don't blink or you'll miss it."

"I don't doubt it," Chris said. "I've lived in California all my life, and I never heard of Drago."

"Neither had I," Karyn said. "We were lucky to find the place. The house has been empty since the old owners died four years ago. Roy fell in love with it."

"What about you, Karyn? How do you like the place?"

"It's all right, I suppose."

"You don't sound convinced."

"I haven't seen it since Roy had it fixed up. Anyway, it *is* quiet and out of the way. That's what we wanted. And yet it's only a two-hour drive from Los Angeles, so Roy can commute easily."

"You won't mind being alone when he comes into L.A.?"

"Why should I? I've got to learn to be by myself sometime." The words came out more sharply than Karyn had intended.

"That's right," Chris said. "It's none of my business, anyway."

They reached the crest of the ridge and the road leveled off for a stretch before descending into the valley on the other side. The air was pungent with the scent of balsam. Karyn reached out and touched Chris's hand.

"Pull over for a minute, can you?"

Just before the road started down Chris eased the Camaro onto the shoulder and parked next to the metal guard rail. Below them lay a narrow valley, thick with evergreens. Where the road straightened along the floor of the valley a dozen or so toylike buildings clustered in a clearing of the forest. Several narrow lanes branched off the main road. They could be seen only faintly through the heavy overgrowth. Here and there along the lanes a tiny house sat on a patch of cleared ground reclaimed from the forest. Although the valley was in shadow, no lights shone in the town of Drago.

"It doesn't look like much from up here, does it?" Karyn said.

Chris did not answer.

"May I have a cigarette?"

He handed her one and lighted it for her.

Karyn took several quick puffs before speaking. "I really do want to talk to someone, Chris. Someone who cares about me as a person, not as a case history to read at the next psychiatric convention."

She mashed the cigarette into the ashtray. When she spoke again the words came out in a rush. "Chris, Roy and I haven't had good sex together since that day. There's nothing wrong physically, but it's just not working. Roy and I have talked and talked about it, and God knows we *do* try. We go to bed, and I want it so much . . . I go through all the motions. That's the trouble, all I'm doing is going through the motions. There's no feeling, and Roy knows it. He can't help but know it—he's not a fool. He's been awfully sweet and patient with me, but I can't expect him to put up with this forever. I just don't seem to be getting any better."

"Did you talk the problem over with your doctor?" Chris asked.

"Oh, hell yes."

"Did he give you any advice?"

"Nothing I couldn't have gotten out of *The Reader's Digest*. Good, sound, logical advice, but I still don't feel anything."

"Give it a while," Chris said. "Two months isn't much time to get over what happened to you."

Karyn nodded distractedly.

"Anyway," Chris went on, "that's what you're moving out here to the woods for, isn't it? Rest and rejuvenation?"

With an encouraging smile, he started the car, pulled back onto the road, and drove down into the valley. As they descended, the mountain loomed up behind and cut off the sun. The air grew cold, and they rolled up the windows. When the road leveled out into the main street of Drago, Chris switched on the headlights against the gathering gloom. They drove slowly along past the buildings, which had a dusty, unused look. There were a couple of stores, a café, a gas station, a tavern, and a theater with an empty marquee. The only sound they heard was the singing of their tires over the pavement.

Karyn shivered slightly in the cool dusk of the tree-lined street. In the back seat Lady whined softly. Karyn reached back without turning around and rubbed the soft fur at the dog's throat.

"Where is everybody?" Chris asked. His eyes ranged along the blank fronts of the buildings.

"I don't know." Karyn shivered again.

"Is your house on this street?"

"No, it's up one of these little cross streets. They all look alike, though, and I'm not sure which it is. We'll have to ask someone."

Chris eased the Camaro along for a hundred yards,

then braked to a stop as a powerful-looking man in kha-
kis and a Stetson appeared from the shadows.

Karyn rolled down her window and smiled at the man.
"Hello, there. I wonder if you could tell us how to get
to the old Fenno house?"

For a moment she thought the man had not heard. He
did not answer her smile, nor did he make any move to
respond. His eyes continued to watch from the shadow
of the Stetson. Then the man came toward them, moving
with a deliberate measured gait. He planted both hands on
the window sill and looked in. Involuntarily, Karyn drew
back in the seat.

"You want the Fenno place?" the man said. His voice
rumbled up from the deep barrel chest.

"Yes. I'm Karyn Beatty. My husband and I are leasing
the house, and I can't remember which of these side
roads it's on."

The man thumbed his hat brim up a fraction, and a
faint smile twitched on his mouth. "Pleased to meet you.
I'm Anton Gadak. I'm sort of the sheriff here in Drago.
Fact is, I'm sort of the whole police force. But then, we
don't need all that much policing." He looked pointedly
past Karyn at Chris.

"This is our friend Chris Halloran. He drove me in
from Los Angeles. My husband is waiting at the house."

Anton Gadak nodded, apparently satisfied. "The Fenno
place is up the last road that turns off to the left, just
before you start up into the hills again."

Karyn thanked him and Chris started away from the
curb. He found the last turnoff with some difficulty. It
was little more than a wide weed-covered path into the
woods.

"As I remember, it's up here about a mile," Karyn
said.

They passed two weathered old houses, dark and
nearly hidden from the road by the brush. At each Chris

looked over at Karyn, who shook her head. They came at last to a small clearing with a white frame cottage trimmed in apple green. A fireplace chimney trailed a ribbon of pale smoke across the slate-gray sky. Lights shone in all the windows, pushing the forest back. Chris pulled onto the clearing and parked behind Roy Beatty's Galaxie.

Karyn clapped her hands delightedly. "What an improvement! You wouldn't believe the dismal brown color the house was when we first came out. And the whole place was strangled with brush and weeds. Roy's done a marvelous job."

Chris got out of the car and walked back to open the trunk. As he brought out Karyn's bags the front door of the little house swung open and Roy Beatty came out. He shielded his eyes against the headlights for a moment, then waved a welcome and hurried toward the car.

Karyn jumped out and ran to his arms. "Roy, it's . . . it's beautiful."

"Didn't I tell you it had possibilities?" said Roy. "Wait till you see the inside."

With his arm around Karyn, Roy walked back to the car. "Come on in, Chris, and take a look at how us rural folk live."

"Thanks, but I've got to get back to the city."

"Are you sure? There's steaks in the freezer, and the martini makings are already set out."

"It's tempting, but I'll pass this time."

"Got a date with a live one?"

Chris smiled and gave a noncommittal wave of his hand. "Bring her out some weekend," Roy said. "We've got an extra bed and plenty of blankets."

"Maybe I'll do that."

Roy hefted Karyn's two suitcases, then looked around, puzzled. "Where's Lady?"

"She's been acting funny," Karyn said. "I don't think she knows what to make of the woods."

At that moment, the dog put her nose out for a tentative sniff of the surroundings, then bounded out of the car and frolicked happily around Roy's feet. He knelt and scratched her ear.

While Roy and Karyn watched the dog, Chris slid into his car and pulled the door closed. Roy walked over and reached through the window to shake his hand.

"Thanks for bringing the family out, buddy," he said. "Sorry you can't stay."

"Maybe next time. I hope the place works out for you, Roy."

"It will," Roy assured him.

Karyn came over and kissed him lightly on the cheek. Chris backed out onto the narrow lane and drove back the way they had come. Soon the glow of the Camaro's tail lights was lost among the trees.

"I wish Chris had stayed for dinner," she said as they started toward the house. "I think he's lonely."

"Are you kidding? A handsome thirty-year-old bachelor with a good-paying job and an apartment at the marina? You call that lonely?"

"You sound a little jealous, mister."

Roy set down one of her bags, and gave her a swat on the bottom. "That's right, I can hardly wait to dump you so I can grow a mustache, buy a Porsche, load up on stereo equipment, and be a swinging bachelor."

Laughing together, they continued up to the front stoop. Roy stood aside and gestured her into the living room.

Karyn started in, then hesitated. She ran her fingers down the surface of the heavy wooden door. Under the fresh green paint a series of deep vertical grooves like scars slashed the panel at about shoulder height.

"What do you suppose made these?" she said.

"Who knows?" Roy shrugged and went on inside.

Karyn followed, thinking about the marks. Absurd

though it was, the angry furrows in the wood suggested only one thing.

Claws.

CHAPTER THREE

~~~~~~

The small living room and the open dining area were spotlessly clean and lit with colorful new lamps. A blaze crackled over logs in the stone fireplace. The dark old furniture that had come with the house had been cleaned, polished, and recovered in bright hues. The floor was freshly sanded and waxed and covered with new rugs. Vases of fresh-cut flowers were everywhere.

Roy Beatty stood back and let Karyn survey the rooms. "Well, what do you think?"

"Roy, it's lovely. I mean it."

Karyn walked down the short hallway and looked into the bedroom. There was new maple furniture and a bright patchwork quilt on the double bed. Across the hall in the bathroom new wood paneling had replaced the scabrous, peeling wallboard. The fixtures were scoured, the air sweetened. Karyn came back out and walked through the dining area, running her fingers over the satiny finish of the heavy oak table. Out in the kitchen everything fairly sparkled. She came back into the living room where Roy waited, unable to conceal his pride.

"It's not Hermosa Terrace," he said, "but cozy, don't you think?"

"Very cozy," she agreed.

"How about a martini to toast our new home?"

"Lovely idea."

Roy went into the kitchen and brought back a bowl of ice, which he set before her on a low table in front of the fireplace. The green hydrant bottle of Tanqueray and the vermouth were already there. As he stirred the cocktails in a tall pitcher Lady began to whine softly and scratch at the baseboard near the front door.

"I think it's time she took a trip outside," Roy said. He crossed the room and held the door open. "Come on, Lady, out."

The dog looked up at him uncertainly, then at Karyn.

"Do you think she'll be all right?" Karyn said.

"Sure. There's no traffic out here, and she won't go far enough from the house to get lost."

Lady crouched lower to the floor, her eyes on Roy.

"Come on, you, *out*," he said again, in a more commanding tone.

The little dog obeyed at last, moving in a cautious sidling manner. Roy closed the door after her. He then selected two hefty logs from the pile on the hearth and laid them on the dwindling fire. They caught immediately. The flames snapped at the pockets of pitch and leaped up the chimney.

Roy sat down again and finished stirring the martinis. He brought out two iced glasses and filled them at the low table. They touched glasses, sipped at the cocktails, and smiled at each other.

"Did you get everything worked out at the office?" Karyn asked.

"It's all taken care of. I've got next year's publication list to go over. When I go into town I'll bring back whatever raw copy there is for editing. There's no reason why technical manuals can't be edited up here in the woods as well as on Wilshire Boulevard. I shouldn't have to make the trip into L.A. more than a couple of times a week, if that often."

Karyn leaned back on the sofa. "Are you *sure* you don't mind being cooped up here away from the city and all our friends?"

"Mind? What's to mind? You think I miss battling through the smog and the freeway traffic twice a day? Listen, this is as much a vacation for me as it is therapy for you."

Karyn squeezed his hand. "You're pretty sweet, you know that?"

"Yeah, I know, but tell me anyway."

"What about some dinner? I'm starved."

"Right. I'll get the steaks going while you build a salad."

"Do we have everything we need?"

"We should have. I stocked up this afternoon at the Safeway over in Pinyon."

"Pinyon?"

"That's the nearest town of any size. It's about twelve miles from here at the tip of Castaic Lake."

"Why didn't you do the shopping in Drago?"

"I guess you didn't get too good a look at the town. There's one general store that's about the size of the cheese section in most supermarkets. They had a few canned goods, a few boxes of cereal, a tiny meat counter, and that was it. Oh, yes, the place doubles as a post office."

"At least we *do* have a post office."

"Not exactly," Roy said with an apologetic grin. "The nearest post office is in Pinyon, but they do bring the Drago mail over once a day to the store."

"And that's where we go to pick up our mail," Karyn said.

"That's it. There's a funny little old lady running the place. You'll have to meet her."

"I hope she's funnier than the sheriff."

"You met Anton Gadak?"

"On the way in. He didn't exactly welcome us with open arms."

"Yeah, well, it probably takes these people a while to warm up to strangers."

"I suppose so." Karyn leaned over and kissed him lightly on the cheek. "You were saying something about steaks?"

They ate together at the big oak dining table while shadows cast by the fire danced across the walls. After dinner they relaxed on the sofa, drinking rich burgundy out of big tulip glasses.

"It seems like a strange little town," Karyn remarked. "What kind of a name is Drago, anyway?"

"I don't know. It's not Spanish or Indian. Has a European sound. Hungarian or something. Tomorrow we can ask in the village. It will give us a chance to meet some of the local people. And we can get some candles to go with this romantic setting."

After she had rinsed off the dinner dishes and stacked them in the sink, she joined Roy back in the living room.

"I wonder what the last people were like," Karyn said, sitting down and lighting a cigarette.

"Who?"

"The people who lived in this house before us. The Fennos."

"The man who handled the lease didn't know much about them," Roy said. "Apparently they were an older couple. Moved out here from somewhere in the East to retire. Weren't here long when they died in some kind of an accident. I didn't get any details."

They both started at the sound of something scraping at the front door.

"Lady," Roy said, relaxing with a little laugh. "We forgot all about her."

He walked over and opened the door. The little dog dashed into the room and across the rug to the couch. There she jumped up and pressed close to Karyn, peering back toward the door with wide brown eyes.

"She looks frightened," Karyn said.

Roy stepped outside and looked both ways in the darkness. "Nothing out here."

He came back inside and closed the door. Lady stayed close to Karyn on the sofa.

They talked for a while about nothing important while the logs in the fireplace burned down to a dusky red, finally collapsing in a shower of sparks.

Roy stretched his arms up over his head and yawned generously. "I don't know about you, but I'm beat. Ready to go to bed?"

Karyn felt her muscles tighten. "Maybe I'll have a nice cup of coffee first. Everything tastes so good up here in the mountains." Even in her own ears the light tone of voice rang false.

Karyn took as long as she could with the coffee. She made herself smile at Roy who sat beside her waiting patiently. "Suddenly I'm tired too. Let's go to bed," she said.

They went into the bedroom and Roy turned back the quilt and the snowy top sheet. Karyn's nerves crawled beneath her skin.

She undressed quickly, feeling sure Roy's eyes were fastened on the bite scar—broken red parentheses on the white skin of her inner thigh. She slipped into bed beside her husband and pulled up the covers. Maybe this time it would be all right.

But it was not all right. As soon as they were together in the big comfortable bed and she felt Roy's hand on her—Roy's gentle, familiar hand—a chill spread from her crotch up and throughout her body. Karyn squeezed her eyes shut and ran through all the mental tricks the doctor had given her to blot out the hateful memory of the rape. She clasped her arms about Roy's well-muscled back and pulled him down on top of her. She kissed him passionately and whispered their special love words in his ear.

She felt his body grow tense against hers. Gently he pulled away.

"Oh, Roy, what's the matter with me?"

"Nothing is the matter with you, except that you keep thinking something's the matter with you."

"I'm so sorry."

"Cut it out. Everything will be fine as long as we don't force it."

She trailed her fingers slowly across his flat stomach. "Can I do something, you know, for you?"

He shifted his body a fraction of an inch away from her. "Never mind, honey. Get some sleep. Everything will work out."

After that they lay together, their bodies touching, their minds miles apart.

Many hours later, in the cold, empty darkness before the dawn, Karyn heard the howling.

CHAPTER FOUR

~~~~~~

Morning came slowly to the valley. The blackness of the bedroom lightened imperceptibly through the shades of gray, and at last a finger of sunlight jabbed through a gap in the curtains. Karyn lay wakeful for a long time waiting for Roy to stir. At last his eyes opened. He looked over at Karyn and smiled.

"Good morning," she said, rolling on her side to kiss him lightly on the mouth. "Sleep well?"

"Sure, I guess so. You?"

"Fine. Except for . . ." She hesitated, not wanting to start the day by complaining.

"Except for what?"

"Did you hear anything last night?"

"Hear what?"

"Something . . . like howling."

"No, I didn't hear a thing."

"Maybe it was the wind," she said.

"That was probably it. Blowing over the chimney."

"Probably."

Roy reached over and patted her hip. "Let's have some breakfast. Afterward we can go in and take a look at the town."

Karyn swung lightly out of bed. "You go ahead and take your shower and I'll start getting things set up in the kitchen."

Together they prepared and ate a breakfast of plump country sausages, eggs over easy, muffins, home-fried potatoes, and coffee. Back in the city they seldom had more than plain toast. The food along with the crisp, piny morning air put them in an excellent mood.

Lady was given a helping of canned dogfood with a fresh egg beaten into it. She ate as hungrily as the two people, and afterward dashed eagerly outside.

"I'll get the car," Roy said.

"Couldn't we walk into town?" Karyn said. "It can't be more than two miles, and it's such a beautiful day."

Roy grinned at her, his old warm grin, and Karyn felt a rush of affection for her husband. "I keep forgetting that you lived in Manhattan," he said. "I've never seen people walk as much as New Yorkers."

"You wouldn't, being a Southern California boy," Karyn replied. "People here take the car to go to the mailbox."

"Speaking of cars—" Roy began.

Karyn held up a hand to stop him. "I promise, darling, I'll take driving lessons first thing when we get back."

"I don't mean to nag," Roy said, "but there are times when it could be important."

"Yes, sir," Karyn said with mock servility. Roy could not hold his stern expression.

They both turned as the little dog dashed in through the open door and skidded to a stop, legs braced, ready to play.

"Lady will enjoy the walk too," Karyn said. "Won't you, girl?"

With Lady running ahead, Karyn and Roy started down the narrow lane toward the village of Drago. They continued past the old houses which, Karyn saw, were gray and crumbling, with sagging boards and blind windows. The yards had long since gone to weeds.

"Why do you suppose the people moved out and just left these old houses to rot?" Karyn remarked uneasily.

"Who knows? Drago isn't exactly a boom town. I guess when people die or move away, nobody comes in to take their place."

When they reached the blacktopped road, the main street of Drago, the dog stopped her forays ahead and stayed close to their feet, her ears up, eyes alert.

Karyn and Roy stopped for a moment. Sunlight filtering through the evergreen boughs gave the town a hazy, unreal appearance. The trees sighed under a gentle breeze. No one moved along the street.

"How many people are supposed to be living here?" Karyn asked. Her voice was hushed, as though she were speaking in a church. Or a cemetery.

"I don't know," Roy answered. "Somewhere between a hundred and two hundred."

"Where do you suppose everybody is?"

"Maybe they sleep late."

"Oh, there's someone now," Karyn said.

Across the street Anton Gadak stood leaning in the doorway of a small shop. His blocky form was half-hidden in shadows. Karyn and Roy crossed the street and approached him.

"Good morning," Roy said. "For a while there we thought the town was closed today."

Gadak touched the brim of his Stetson and nodded to Karyn. He spoke to Roy. "You'll find us pretty quiet here in Drago."

"That's fine with us," Roy said. "We're pretty quiet

ourselves. Are there stores open?"

"You can buy groceries and most anything else down the street at the Jolivets'." Gadak jerked a thumb toward the narrow shop behind him. "And knicknacks you can get in here." He touched his hat brim again and swung off down the street without waiting for further conversation.

Roy looked after him, shaking his head. "I thought he'd never shut up."

"How do you suppose he got to be sheriff?"

"I think it's an honorary title," Roy said. "The town of Drago is not incorporated."

"Well, shall we check out the 'knicknacks'?" Karen suggested pointing to the shop. "They may have candles."

There was no sign identifying the shop. A curtain was pulled across the show window, and the glass in the door was too dark to see through, giving the place an abandoned look. Roy thumbed the latch and pushed the door open. The clear tinkle of a tiny bell sounded inside. He let Karyn precede him and told Lady to stay put outside.

The interior of the shop was cluttered and dimly lit, but seemed quite clean. A faint scent of sandalwood hung in the air, mingling with the even fainter hint of herbs. A glass-fronted counter ran along one wall of the shop. All around were shelves and small tables filled with colorful and useless objects of the kind people like to give as presents, but seldom buy for themselves. There were china figurines, embroidered pillows, hurricane lamps, ceramic dishes, ornate vases, lace handkerchiefs, costume jewelry, and a collection of boxes and bottles with contents unknown.

"Wonder where the proprietor is," Roy murmured.

A soft green curtain covering a doorway at the rear of the shop moved, and Karyn and Roy looked that way. The curtain parted in the center, sliding along the rod on silent rings, and a young woman stepped through.

The woman's hair was raven black, and soft with glinting highlights. Her eyes slanted just barely, and were a pale green that seemed lit from within. She wore a loose satiny garment that covered her from throat to ankles. When she moved it touched her in a way that revealed the lithe body underneath.

"Hello," the woman said in a smoky voice. "I wondered when you would be in." Her pale-green eyes were trained full on Roy, ignoring Karyn.

"Well, hello," Roy said in a tone Karyn barely recognized. "Were you expecting us?"

"I saw you in the village yesterday. I knew you would be here soon. How may I serve you?"

An old grandfather's clock behind the counter ticked four times before Roy answered. "Candles," he blurted. Then, more composed, "We wanted to buy some candles. We've moved into what I guess is called the old Fenno house."

"Yes, I know," said the black-haired woman. Noting Karyn's quizzical look she added, "In a small town there are few secrets. My name is Marcia Lura."

"I'm Roy Beatty, and this is my wife, Karyn."

"You *do* have candles?" Karyn said. It came out more sharply than she intended, but the other woman did not seem to notice.

"Oh, yes, Mrs. Beatty, I have candles of all kinds." Marcia Lura turned to face Karyn. In the way she moved and the sharp contrast of pale-green eyes and midnight hair there could be a powerful attraction for a man. Was there also a challenge? Karyn wondered.

"We don't need anything elaborate," Roy said. "Just something for the dinner table. Something romantic." He gave Karyn a quick grin, but his gaze quickly returned to Marcia Lura.

"I understand," Marcia said with a slow smile. "I'm sure I have something that will please you."

Karyn kept her smile in place, but behind it she ground her teeth. Never had she considered herself a jealous woman, but now it infuriated her the way this woman directed her conversation to Roy, and seemed to put double meanings on everything she said. Maybe, Karyn thought, the double meanings were in her own mind. In any case, she did not intend to be upstaged.

"Do you live here in Drago?" Karyn asked, moving a step closer to her husband and touching his arm possessively.

"Yes, I have rooms right here behind the shop. There's not much space, but being alone, I don't need much," Marcia said with a smile. Her mouth was wide and full, a pale-pink shade that might or might not have been achieved with lipstick. "If you will step over this way I'll show you what I have in candles."

They settled for half a dozen slim green candles with a pair of plain glass holders. Not until Roy was paying the woman did Karyn notice that the candles matched the color of her eyes. When they left the shop Karyn felt a vast relief at being back in the fresh air. She reached down and absently scratched Lady behind the ear.

"Striking woman, wasn't she," Karyn said as casually as possible.

"Who? Oh, yes, I suppose you could say she was."

"You didn't notice, I suppose."

Roy snaked an arm around Karyn's waist and pulled her close to him. "Hell, yes, I noticed. Want to make something of it?"

Karyn smiled, happy to have her husband's full attention once again. "Maybe," she said. "Once we get home and get those romantic candles lit."

"Do we need any groceries?" Roy asked.

"I don't think so. You did a pretty good job of shopping yesterday. We could use bread and some milk."

"We can pick that up down at the Jolivets'. He doesn't say much, but she's a character. Anyway, I want you to know where the telephone is."

Karyn stopped suddenly and looked at him. "What telephone?"

"Our telephone. Didn't you notice that there isn't one in the house?"

"No, as a matter of fact, I didn't."

"There are no wires strung out there. Anytime we have to make a call we use the phone at Jolivet's store."

"When we go rural, we don't mess around," Karyn said.

They walked on up the street to a false-front wooden building with a faded sign reading *Jolivet's General Merchandise*. Inside, the store seemed to be stocked indiscriminately with hardware, clothes, and groceries. It had probably looked the same for the last forty years.

Standing at an ancient cash register was a round-faced little woman with a snub nose, rimless glasses, and a bright smile. "Hi, Roy," she said with easy familiarity. "I see the little woman got in all right."

"That's right," Roy said. "This is my wife, Karyn. Oriole Jolivet."

"My, you're pretty as a picture," said Oriole, coming around the counter and taking Karyn's hands. "I just knew a handsome devil like Roy would have a looker for a wife."

"Well, thank you," Karyn said, a little embarrassed, but flattered as well.

"That's my husband, Etienne, over there by the meat case," Oriole said.

A long-faced man looked up from the tray of chops he was arranging and gave Karyn a sad smile.

"You're the first new folks to move into Drago in quite a spell," Oriole told them. "Hope we'll be seein' you around from time to time."

"I'm sure you will," Karyn said.

"No need to wait till you have to buy something, just come on by anytime you feel like chewin' the fat."

"I'll do that," Karyn said.

"Good, good. Do you like coffee?"

"I love coffee."

Oriole's smile got even brighter. "That's the kind of talk I like to hear. Yes, indeed, you and me are goin' to get along fine, Karyn. Now you wait right there and I'll go out back and pour us all a cup."

"I don't want you to go to any trouble—"

"No trouble at all, honey. Be back in a jiffy."

Oriole bustled out and returned in a moment carrying a tray laden with cups of dark, rich coffee and thick slices of cinnamon-sprinkled coffee cake. Karyn sipped the coffee and chatted with Oriole while Roy prowled around the store. For the first time since arriving in Drago she felt at ease.

When they had finished the last of the coffee and cake, Roy bought a loaf of bread and two quarts of milk. He put the candles in the bag with the groceries and they left the Jolivets' store.

Lady, who seemed to sense that they were going home now, bounded off down the street. Watching the dog, Karyn touched Roy's arm and pointed toward one of the old houses. There a boy and girl of about twelve stood motionless in the front yard watching them. Their faces were grave, their eyes shadowed. A woman came out onto the porch and said something. The children turned silently and went inside.

"You know," Karyn said, "those are the first children I've seen in this town."

"The rest of them are probably in school."

"Where? I haven't seen anything in Drago that looks like a school."

"Maybe they go over to Pinyon," Roy said. "Does it matter?"

"I guess not," Karyn said, "but it does seem odd."

CHAPTER FIVE

~~~~~~

That night in bed Karyn gave the finest acting performance of her life. She twisted and moaned under her husband; she dug her nails into his back. She caressed him with her hands and with her mouth. She heaved her body to meet his thrusts and clamped her legs around his waist. She cried out words of passion as she felt his climax burst inside her.

And she felt nothing.

She could not be sure if Roy knew. He gripped her with his strong, square hands and tongued her ear and said all the right things as he approached orgasm, but Karyn was not sure that he believed her response. At least, she told herself, he had climaxed. Her performance was not wasted.

Afterward he rolled over and slept. Karyn lay beside him trying to sleep too. But as the minutes ticked into hours she gave it up and lay waiting, listening. She knew it would come, as surely as death. And it did come. The distant ululation. The mournful sinister night cry. The howling.

After that she slept fitfully, waking up time and again to listen breathlessly to the night. Finally she came awake with a start to find that it was light and Roy was gone from the bed. She could smell coffee perking in the kitchen, and hurried to join her husband.

That day, and the next, and the next, Karyn and Roy did not go into the village of Drago. They stayed close to the little house, walking on the trails in the forest and delighting in the birds and wild flowers. Lady loved these outings. She would rush joyfully ahead barking officiously at anything that moved, as though clearing the path for her people. Although Karyn and Roy kept up the pretense of enjoying each other, each was occupied with thoughts that could not be shared.

In the evenings they played cribbage or backgammon. Having no television set, they rediscovered the radio. Sometimes Karyn would read from the stack of paperbacks she had brought from the city while Roy worked at the kitchen table going over the list of his company's technical publications.

At night Karyn tried to let go during sex, but it became harder all the time to pretend she was enjoying it. Roy's lovemaking became perfunctory, and at last he merely kissed her goodnight and turned away. Then while he slept Karyn would lie on her back, her muscles taut, and stare into the dark.

Every night now, the howling came. Karyn no longer asked Roy if he heard it. He never seemed to. Karyn was afraid that if she talked about it he would say it was all in her head. She knew better. Something was out there. Something.

By the end of the first week Karyn had dug out the bottle containing the remaining Seconals the doctor in

Los Angeles had prescribed when she came home from the hospital. She had never liked taking pills, but at last she was able to sleep soundly.

Roy began to walk in the forest by himself. His excuse was that he wanted to gather wood for the fireplace but Karyn knew there was all the wood they needed within fifty yards of the house. The real reason had to be that he wanted to get away from her.

She became convinced of it the day of Roy's first trip into Los Angeles. Although he made a show of reluctance to leave their wilderness paradise, his eagerness was not hard to read. She watched the Ford disappear down the narrow lane with an increasing sense of fear and uneasiness.

The day was cool with a high overcast. Karyn vowed to pull herself out of her funk. She put on a heavy sweater and took Lady for a long walk through the woods. For a city girl, she had a remarkable sense of direction, and there was never any problem finding her way back.

Returning home around noon, she washed the walls and windows, even though they didn't need it. She fixed herself a sandwich, fed the dog, and shuffled through the books without finding one she wanted to read. She began looking up the road for Roy long before he was due to return.

When at last he drove into the yard, Karyn ran out to meet him and they hugged each other enthusiastically and walked back to the house arm in arm.

Karyn had prepared a small roast for their meal. It came out perfectly—crispy brown on the outside, pink and tender within. The candles provided an intimate glow, and the talk came easy. It was almost the way it had been before their trouble started.

After dinner Karyn fed Lady and let her outside while Roy poured their brandy. They moved into the living room and sat close together by the fireplace. Their legs touched, and for the first time in months Karyn felt a surge of desire for her husband.

"Roy," she said, "let's go to bed."

"Sleepy already?"

She shook her head, holding the warm pressure of her thigh against him. "Nope."

Roy looked at her closely for a moment, then took her into his arms. He kissed her. She returned the kiss with feeling. Everything about him—his hands on her back, the taste of his mouth, even the short stubble of beard—excited her.

"Let's not waste any more time," he said. They stood up together and he led her into the bedroom.

When they were lying together, Karyn rolled onto her side to face him. Roy's hand roved down across her rib cage and up over the swell of her hip. She reached down for his sex and found him erect and hard. The touch of him in her hand was good. His fingers trailed down across her flat stomach and into the blond fluff of pubic hair. She felt herself open willingly and go moist under his touch.

Oh, God, said a part of Karyn's mind, *let it be good this time. Let it be right, the way it was.*

Roy was kissing her breast, teasing the erect nipple with his tongue. His hand was up between her legs, stroking, massaging. Karyn was ready for him. As ready as she would ever be. Then she heard it.

The howling.

Not far off in the woods this time, but close outside. Close, deep-throated, and cold as death.

"Roy!" she said, sitting up in bed.

"I heard it," he said. He pulled himself up beside her, but his voice did not reflect the urgency that Karyn felt.

Roy's hand moved between her legs. His head dipped again to her breast.

"What was it?" Karyn said. She was whispering without knowing why.

"I don't know. An owl." His tone took on an edge of impatience.

"Not an owl," she said.

"Who cares? Come on, Karyn, lie down."

Obediently Karyn lay back on the sheet. She tried hard to recover the mood of a few moments before, but the terrible howling still sounded in her brain. How could Roy ignore it?

His head moved lower on her body. She could feel his tongue tracing a moist line across her navel and on down . . .

Abruptly it was not her husband kissing her down there, it was that horrible other thing. The teeth.

With a startled cry she drew away from him.

He pulled himself up. "What?"

Karyn reached out to him, trying to make her touch affectionate, though she still felt the unreasoning revulsion. "I'm sorry, Roy. I—I don't think I can."

"But just a minute ago—"

"I know," she said quickly. "I know, Roy, but now I can't."

"Jesus," he said through clenched teeth, and turned away from her. His broad naked back was like a wall in the middle of the bed.

"Please, darling," she said, "be patient with me for a little while longer."

He gave her an unconvincing pat on the shoulder. "Sure, Karyn, it's all right. I'm just keyed up after driving out from the city."

But it was not all right, and they both knew it. Karyn's throat filled up with words she wanted to say to her husband but could not: *I'm sorry, dear, I was all ready and in the mood, and then something howled outside. No, it was not an owl. And after that the only picture in my mind was that filthy animal with his hands up in me and his teeth biting me and then . . . and then . . .*

Karyn forced her mind back from the brink of hysteria,

and at last fell into a shallow sleep.

In the morning she was the first one up. She combed out her hair and went into the kitchen. She would prepare a lovely breakfast for Roy—ham-and-cheese omelet with hot muffins, and rich black coffee. But first she had to feed the dog. She took a can of Alpo from the cupboard, then wondered why Lady did not come trotting in at the sound of the can on the countertop. Then she remembered that no one had let her back in last night. Karyn went to open the front door. The dog was not in sight.

Karyn stepped outside and called the dog's name. The forest was unusually silent on this gray, damp day, the only sound the dripping of moisture from the tree branches. Karyn called again and walked all around the yard. Nothing answered.

She went back inside and into the bedroom, where Roy sat on the edge of the bed pulling on a pair of denim pants.

"Lady's not here," she said. "We forgot to let her in last night. Now I can't find her. She doesn't answer." Karyn sensed the rising pitch of her voice, but she did not try to control it. Concern for the dog was an acceptable outlet for the other tangled emotions that she was not ready to examine.

"I'll go take a look," Roy replied. He went outside, whistling and calling for the little dog. He made several forays into the woods, calling louder, and came back with his jeans wet from the damp brush.

"She's probably off exploring somewhere," he said without conviction.

"Roy, do you think something's happened to her?"

"What could happen? We've been here over a week. Lady knows her way around by now. She'll come home when she gets hungry."

Karyn caught the irritability just beneath his words. She said, "I guess we might as well eat breakfast."

She had lost all enthusiasm for the omelet. While she

cooked it, Karyn left the front door open. From time to time each of them would look over that way.

Afterward Roy went to work editing his manuscripts. Karyn sat in a chair by the window with a book open on her lap. She tried to read, but the printed words would not register on her mind. When it was almost noon she could sit still no longer.

"Roy, I think we should go out and look for her. She may be hurt and can't get back to us."

Roy looked over at her, and Karyn could see that he was not as unconcerned as he acted. "All right," he said.

The sun was out now, high and pale, but warm enough to dry off the forest. Roy and Karyn walked the trails that interlaced the surrounding woods. Some were so dim and overgrown that they were hardly there. Others showed signs of recent use.

Roy went in one direction, Karyn in another. She concentrated on looking down as she walked, scanning the ground along both sides of each trail. She saw nothing.

When Roy came upon her suddenly walking from the opposite direction, she started and gave a little squeal of surprise.

He reached out and grasped her arm gently. "No luck?" She shook her head.

"Roy, let's try going into town."

"What for?"

"Maybe Lady got confused and went that way. Maybe somebody saw her. It wouldn't hurt to ask. It's better than sitting in that house and waiting to hear her bark, or see her come running home." Karyn turned away so Roy would not see the sudden tears. "Damn, how stupid it is to let a little animal become such a part of your life. *Stupid*."

Roy put his arms around Karyn and held her for a moment.

They did not talk during the short drive. There was

no sign of the dog in the roadway or in the brush along-side.

Once they were in the village Roy pulled over to the side and turned to Karyn while the engine idled. "What now?"

Karyn looked up and down the deserted street, con-fused. "How . . . how about that sheriff or whatever he is, Anton Gadak? Maybe he would know if anybody has seen Lady."

The words were barely out of her mouth when the broad figure of Anton Gadak appeared up the street, angling across the blacktop toward their car. Roy shut off the engine and got out on the driver's side. Karyn came around and stood beside him.

Gadak put two fingers to the brim of his Stetson. "Afternoon, folks. Haven't seen you for a few days. Everything all right?"

"Everything's fine," Roy began automatically, then corrected himself. "No, the truth is we've got a problem."

"Problem?" Gadak waited politely.

When Roy hesitated, Karyn spoke up. "It's our little dog. We left her out last night, and this morning she's missing." Even as she spoke, Karyn thought how trivial it must sound.

"Sorry to hear that."

"We wondered if she might have found her way to town somehow."

"If she did, I ain't heard about it," Gadak said. "Folks in Drago don't keep pets much, so they'd most likely notice your dog if she came in this way. I'll ask around, and keep an eye out myself."

"Thanks," Roy said. "We'd appreciate it."

"No trouble."

As the big man was about to turn away, Karyn stopped him. "Mr. Gadak, are there any large animals around here that might have . . . harmed her?"

"Large animals?" Gadak repeated.

"Last night, and on other nights, I've heard something in the woods. A howling."

Gadak pulled at his lower lip and looked down at Karyn. His eyes were shaded by the hat brim. "A howling, you say. Coyote, maybe. Sure, could have been a coyote. Been a few of them seen hereabouts. They'll carry off a small animal now and again. How big was this dog of yours?"

"About so high," Roy said, flattening his hand at about knee level.

"Kinda big for a coyote to take on," Gadak said, "but maybe it was hungry."

"It was not a coyote," Karyn said firmly.

The big man turned his shadowed eyes back to her. "Eh, what's that?"

"The thing I heard howling in the woods. It was no coyote."

"Come on, Karyn," Roy said. "How can you be sure?"

She turned on her husband. "You heard it. You heard the howling last night. Did that sound like a coyote to you?"

Roy's eyes shifted uneasily. "How would I know? I'm a city boy. The only coyotes I ever hear are on *Wild Kingdom*."

"All right," Karyn persisted, "but that howling last night, that didn't sound like any coyote on television—or any other place."

"Maybe an owl," Roy offered.

"Could be," Gadak remarked, scratching his chin. "The woods has a lot of peculiar sounds at night. 'Specially for folks from the city. You'll get used to it."

"I doubt it," Karyn said quietly. She walked around the car and got in.

Anton Gadak spoke to Roy in a confidential tone, but the words came clearly to Karyn through the open window. "I'll ask around about your dog, Mr. Beatty, but I want to be honest with you. I think it's gone for good. Take my word for it, that was a coyote your missus heard. They can tear up a small animal in a hurry when they get hold of one."

Roy got in and turned the car back toward their house. Karyn kept her eyes straight ahead, but she could see Roy glancing over at her.

Without looking at him, she said in a firm voice, "It was no coyote."

CHAPTER SIX

That night Roy did not even try to make love to Karyn. He stayed up long after she went to bed, working, he said. When he finally came silently into the bedroom he was careful not to wake her and immediately went to sleep.

The night after that, Karyn wore her nightgown to bed. It broke a years-long habit of sleeping in the nude. Roy came to bed late again and did not even notice.

The next morning Roy acted especially cheerful, but obviously something was on his mind. After more than a year of marriage Karyn knew the man well enough to wait until he was ready to tell her about it. During his second cup of coffee he did.

"Uh, look, honey, something's come up with the manuscripts I brought home."

"Oh?"

"I've run into some problems that just can't be solved without getting together with the writer. So it looks like I'm going to have to take a run into Los Angeles."

"Today?"

"Well, yes, the sooner the better. You'll be all right?"

"Of course."

"Is there anything I can do for you before I go?"

"I'm not an invalid, Roy."

"I hate to go, but it's one of those things."

Roy dabbed at his mouth and stood up, anxious to be on his way, but trying not to show it. He gathered up the manuscripts he said were giving him trouble and took them out to the car. Karyn walked out with him. She kissed him goodbye, then turned away and walked back to the house as he drove away. When she was back inside Karyn sat down and cried for twenty minutes.

Then, as abruptly as she had started, she stopped crying. She went into the bathroom and washed her face. A bleary, red-eyed image looked back at her from the mirror.

"You look like hell," Karyn said. She soaked a cloth with cool water and patted her face with it.

"How do you expect me to look?" her image seemed to answer. "Sitting around in a house in the middle of the woods with a husband who has turned into a stranger and trying to pretend there's nothing the matter. How would anybody look?"

She took up a brush and began energetically stroking her hair. When her hair had achieved a shimmery golden glow Karyn went back into the living room and sat down in the chair by the window. She picked up a paperback novel.

After a little while Karyn tossed the book aside. She recognized a new emotion building in her. Anger. She had seethed inside since the other day when Roy and that so-called sheriff Anton Gadak had been so patronizing to her with their smug explanations of the howling.

Coyote like hell! Owl my foot! Something else howled in the woods around Drago. Karyn decided suddenly that she was going to find out what.

She went into the bedroom and changed into jeans and a suede jacket. She put on a comfortable pair of moccasins and set off walking toward the village. When she reached Drago's main street she was surprised to see that there were several people out walking. No one she recognized, but at least it was evidence that there were other people living here.

She looked over at the little shop run by Marcia Lura. Door closed and dark, curtain across the window as usual. She wondered how the woman could attract enough customers to keep the place open. Or maybe her real business was in the back room. Karyn grinned wickedly.

For that matter, nothing in Drago seemed to do much business. Karyn walked by the open door of a tavern. Inside a solitary customer sat at the bar with a glass of beer in front of him. He looked out at Karyn, his face expressionless.

She continued past the boarded-up theater with its empty marquee. A faded poster tacked behind a glassless frame advertised a motorcycle movie that must have been ten years old.

She crossed the street to Jolivet's General Merchandise. At least there she could count on finding some life and a friendly face.

Oriole Jolivet bustled around the counter to greet her. The little woman wore a wide smile and her eyes twinkled behind the lenses of her glasses.

"Karyn, for gosh sakes, I about decided you'd up and left us."

"Nothing like that," Karyn said. "We've just been staying close to home."

"You ever find your little dog?"

"No."

"Aw, that's too bad. Something like that can really get a person down. How's Roy? Did he come in with you?"

"He had to go into Los Angeles today."

"Oh. You come in for shoppin' or for a visit?"

"For a visit, really, if I'm not taking you away from business."

"That'll be the day. You and me will have us a nice hen party. You're not in any hurry, are you?"

"No, not really."

"Good. I'll put on a fresh pot of coffee. Do you play cards?"

"Roy and I play cribbage sometimes."

"I don't know that one," Oriole said. "How about gin rummy?"

"I used to know how to play that," Karyn said doubtfully, "but it's been a long time."

"Don't worry, it'll come back to you. Just like riding a bicycle." Oriole started back around the counter and beckoned for Karyn to follow. "Come on out to the back. We'll play for half a cent a point, okay? Cards are no fun unless you play for money."

"Half a cent a point is fine," Karyn said, laughing. "You'd better go easy on me, though. I only have about three dollars with me."

"Shoot, I'll trust you for anything over that." Oriole laughed.

As she followed Oriole to the back room of the store, Karyn saw for the first time that Etienne Jolivet was standing silently off at one side of the counter. He gave her a faint smile and nodded. Karyn nodded back and wondered why the man made her uncomfortable.

In the cozy back room Oriole put a big pot of coffee on the stove and cleared off an old kitchen table for their game. She produced a worn deck of cards, a pad of paper, and a yellow stub of pencil.

"The first hand'll be just for practice," Oriole said,

"so you can get the hang of it before we start playing for real."

An hour later Karyn was down $2.80, and Oriole was enjoying herself immensely. Oriole was an aggressive player, if not overly shrewd. Karyn's mind was not on the game.

"You've lived here a long time, haven't you, Oriole?" she asked as the other woman carefully added up the score of the last hand.

"All my life."

"I was wondering . . ." Karyn hesitated, unsure how to proceed.

Oriole looked up and her bright little eyes met Karyn's. "Anything at all you want to know about what goes on in Drago, I'm the one can tell you. Not that all that *much* goes on here."

Karyn smiled in agreement. "It's not really town gossip I was after. I was just wondering . . . well, for one thing, why aren't there any pets in Drago? The sheriff said the people here didn't keep many animals, but I haven't seen a single dog or cat on the street."

Oriole scratched thoughtfully at her nose. "Guess I never thought much about it. Let me see, there's some people named Hemphill on the other side of town from you folks. They keep chickens. Used to, anyway."

"That's not quite what I meant," Karyn said.

"Never cared much for dogs and cats myself," Oriole said.

"Maybe when you're out here closer to nature you don't feel the need to have an animal in the house."

"Maybe that's it." Oriole scooped up the cards and began to shuffle.

"Is there much wildlife in the woods around here?" Karyn asked, keeping it casual.

"We see deer sometimes. Raccoons. Chipmunks, squirrels. That's about it."

"Nothing . . . dangerous?"

"Lordy, no. If you start climbin' the mountains you might run into rattlesnakes, but you won't find them in the woods. It's too cool and damp for rattlesnakes."

"What about coyotes?"

"Well, now, I suppose there could be a coyote wander in through the pass once in a while. You get into the high desert just the other side of the mountains, and they got coyotes over there. Why?"

"I've heard something in the woods at night. Howling. You know Lady, our dog, has disappeared. I wondered if something out there could have got her. Maybe even a wolf?"

"Well, I don't know nothing about wolves." Oriole began dealing the cards, snapping each one firmly down on the table.

"I'd like to find out more," Karyn persisted. "Is there a library? Somewhere I could get books?"

"Not in Drago. Nearest library's over in Pinyon. If you want to call them, they'll send your books over with the mail. Tell 'em you know me and it'll be all right."

"Thanks, Oriole. If I can use your phone, I think I'll do that right now."

"In the middle of our game?"

"I'll be right back. This business has been on my mind, and I'll feel a lot better about it when I've at least done something."

"Okay, help yourself. The phone's out on the counter next to the cash register. I'll heat up the coffee."

Through the operator, Karyn got the number of the library in Pinyon. The librarian there, a Mr. Upshaw, apparently had little to do to keep him busy, and was eager to help Karyn find the kind of books she was looking for, and he said he'd be glad to send them over. They settled on *The Wolf* by L. David Mech, *Never Cry Wolf* by Farley Mowat, and *World of the Wolf* by Russell J. Rutter. All were of recent publication, and all dealt with the wolf in its natural state. For good measure, Karyn asked for the *National Geographic* book on North American mammals.

Karyn and Oriole played gin for another hour, during which Karyn lost another two dollars. Oriole cheerfully accepted an I.O.U. and said she hoped they could make their card game a regular thing. Karyn said she hoped so too—if she could afford it—but really was relieved to get away. Oriole Jolivet was cheerful company but she had hardly anything besides gin rummy to talk about.

Karyn took her time walking back to the house. Rationally she had given up hope of ever seeing Lady again. Still, sometimes she would start at a sudden sound from the woods, thinking it was the bark of a small dog. But it was always something else. Or nothing at all.

CHAPTER SEVEN

~~~~~~

When Karyn came within sight of the house she was surprised to see the Galaxie already parked in front. She had expected Roy to prolong the trip to Los Angeles at least until dark. She was also surprised at her indifference to seeing him. It had never been like that before. Unconsciously she slowed her steps as she neared the house.

In their year of marriage Karyn had known only pleasure in being with Roy. Now after he had made excuses for leaving her, she found herself wishing he had stayed away longer. She walked on slowly toward the house.

Roy was moody and distant in his greeting. Since Karyn was not anxious to talk either, she did not press him. They ate an early dinner, preoccupied with their own thoughts. After dinner they sat apart in the living room and pretended to read.

They both started at the sudden crunch of automobile tires on the gravel outside. Roy shot Karyn a questioning look. She shook her head.

There was a knock at the door, and Roy crossed the room quickly to answer it.

Out on the small porch stood a woman carrying a shopping bag. She was tall and thin, with a bony, big-featured face. Her gray hair was indifferently cut; she wore a shapeless tweed suit and heavy-rimmed glasses. The woman smiled at Roy. She had a good smile that softened the lines of her face.

"Is this where Mrs. Beatty lives?"

Karyn moved in beside Roy. "I'm Karyn Beatty."

The woman's smile took in both of them. "Pleased to meet you. My name is Inez Polk. I live over in Pinyon and I happened to be in the library today while Al Upshaw was getting the books together for you."

Roy turned to Karyn. "What books?"

"I called the library in Pinyon today from the Jolivets'," Karyn explained quickly. She turned back to the thin woman.

"I was intrigued by your selection of books," said Inez Polk, "so I offered to drive over here tonight and drop them off."

"It was kind of you to take the trouble," Karyn said.

"No trouble at all. I'm glad for the excuse to meet you. The fact is I get bored to death sometimes over in Pinyon. I teach English there to junior high school students who consider it just another dead language. I'll grab any chance I get to talk to somebody new and interesting."

Inez Polk looked from Karyn to Roy and back again. "If I'm interrupting something, please say so. I appreciate frankness."

"You're not interrupting a thing," Karyn said. "Please come in. Can I get you a cup of coffee? Or a drink?"

"Have you any wine?"

"Burgundy?"

"A glass of burgundy would be nice." Inez took the four books Karyn had asked for and stacked them on the low table in front of the sofa.

Roy leaned down and fanned the books so he could read the titles. He looked quizzically at Karyn. "Wolves?"

Karyn walked past him into the dining alcove, where she poured two glasses of wine from a decanter. "Yes, wolves," she said shortly. "Would you like some wine, Roy?"

"No, thanks, I think I'll get a little exercise. Take a walk before it gets dark." Roy brushed Karyn's cheek with his lips, said goodbye to Inez, and left the house hastily. Like a man set free, Karyn thought.

She carried the wine back into the living room and sat down on the sofa with Inez. In a very short time the two women were chatting warmly. Inez Polk was intelligent and witty, and shared a surprising number of Karyn's interests and opinions. It had been a long time since Karyn had felt completely relaxed with a stranger. By the time she refilled the wineglasses they were fast friends.

"So what is it with you and the wolves?" Inez said, getting around to her reason for coming.

"You won't laugh?"

"Try me," Inez said. Her expression was dead serious.

Karyn told her about the howling in the woods; how it was far off at first, and quite close the night Lady had disappeared. She told Inez about Roy's skepticism and the sheriff's explanation that it was coyotes.

"And you think there's a wolf out there?" Inez asked.

"I don't know. It sounded like a wolf to me. If that's what got my dog, it had to be as big as a wolf. Lady was no fighter, but I don't believe a coyote would attack her."

"And nobody else has mentioned a wolf?"

"No."

"Mm-hmm. Well, maybe there's a clue in those books?" Both Karyn and Inez were quick scan-readers. They divided the library books and went through them, and soon they had learned more about wolves than they really wanted to know.

From the several species discussed they chose the gray, or timber wolf, *Canis lupus,* as the most likely. This wolf, they read, was the largest found in America—as big as five feet long, including eighteen inches of tail. Some huge specimens had been found in Canada weighing 175 pounds.

Wolves were fierce fighters and exceptionally intelligent, with a diet consisting primarily of smaller animals, but when hunting in packs they could pull down prey much larger than themselves.

The most significant fact the women found was that, except for a few hundred hanging on in the forests of northern Michigan, Minnesota, and Wisconsin, there were no wild wolves left in the United States.

"What do you think then, Inez? *Could* it have been a coyote I heard? Or an owl, for God's sake?"

The thin woman was silent for a minute while she appeared to organize her thoughts. Finally she said, "No, it wasn't any coyote. Or an owl, either."

"Was it in my head, then?"

"No, you heard something, all right."

Karyn studied the other woman for a moment. "You never did tell me why my ordering books about wolves brought you out here tonight. You have some idea what this is all about, don't you?"

"Yes," Inez said slowly. "I have an idea."

"Well, come on, let's hear it."

"Let me tell you a little about myself first. I am thirty-nine years old, never been married, and live alone with my potted plants, which I do *not* talk to, no matter how great the temptation. Every summer I take a trip somewhere alone, meet nobody worth knowing, and come back alone. I read a lot and I have a good collection of classical records."

"Inez, I—" Karyn began.

"No, I am not making a bid for sympathy. I like my life the way it is. Aside from a certain lack of intellectual stimulation, I like living in Pinyon. However, people there think I'm a little odd. Not dangerous odd, but kind of amusing odd."

"What makes you think so"—Karyn said.

"You haven't heard it all yet," Inez interrupted. "For one thing, I used to be a nun."

"A nun?" Karyn repeated.

"Yes, I was a Carmelite. There are quite a few of us failed nuns around today. Unlike most of the others, I didn't leave because of any argument with the Church. In my case it was a personal matter."

Karyn studied the angular woman and tried to visualize her in the traditional nun's habit. Inez simply did not have the round, soft face that one associated with the cloister.

"You're not going to tell me I don't look like a nun?" Inez said, smiling.

Karyn laughed. "As a matter of fact, that's just what I was thinking. Anyway, you were telling me about why you are interested in wolves."

"That's the point I'm leading up to. My interest is not exactly in wolves. You see, I've lived in Pinyon for eleven years, and with a lot of spare time I made a kind of hobby out of local history. Before long I noticed a strange pattern of occurrences in and around Drago. I was intrigued because the pattern seemed to tie in with my other hobby."

"Which is?" Karyn prompted.

Inez drew a deep breath before she answered. "*Diabolus*."

"The devil?"

"You think it's an unusual study for a former nun? Let me tell you, Karyn, that a belief in God requires a

counterbelief in Satan. You must know your enemy before
you can defeat him."

Karyn stared in amazement. "All right, Inez," she said,
hesitantly, making an effort at reason, "but what has . . .
Diabolus to do with me and Drago? Are you saying it's
the Devil who is howling in the woods?"

"No, not the Devil himself." Inez Polk's eyes fell away
for a moment, then returned, bright behind their lenses,
to meet Karyn's gaze. "I think," she said, "that Drago has
a werewolf."

CHAPTER EIGHT

Karyn stared at Inez for a full ten seconds after her shocking suggestion, waiting for some indication that she was joking.

"You're serious, aren't you?" Karyn said finally.

"Deadly serious. Karyn, before you close your mind, please hear me out. Do you know anything about werewolves?"

"Do you mean lycanthropy?"

"No, that's just what I don't mean. Lycanthropy is a disease, a form of mental illness in which the victim imagines himself to be a wolf. He acts like a wolf, losing the power of speech, running around on all fours, growling, and eating raw meat."

"But isn't that what a werewolf is, really?"

"No. A werewolf is a human being who actually, physically, changes into a wolf."

Karyn shook her head. "Inez, I just can't relate to this. We're two grown, reasonably intelligent women. And here we sit discussing werewolves as calmly as though we were talking about fruit flies." Karyn continued very slowly, reasonably. "Inez, you were a nun. As far as I know you're still a Catholic. How can you say these things?"

"Nothing I have said is contrary to the precepts of the Church. If I accept the existence of God as Good, I must also accept the existence of Evil. That's capital-E Evil. Call it whatever you want to—Satan, the Devil, the Antichrist."

"Do you mean that werewolves and the Devil are one and the same?"

"No. The werewolf is a servant of the Devil. No one becomes a werewolf by chance. It's like witchcraft. In return you pledge your everlasting soul."

"People willingly become werewolves?"

"Once it was not at all uncommon. In the Middle Ages life could be an ugly, painful existence if you were very poor, and the price of your soul did not seem too much to pay for the powers of the werewolf."

"But today surely there can't be people still making deals with the Devil."

"Not many, I imagine. Not in the old way."

"Then where would a modern werewolf come from?"

"The curse is passed on to succeeding generations. Unless the line is wiped out, there is no end."

"So to be a werewolf, you either have to make a pact with the Devil, or have a werewolf for a parent." Karyn was trying to be sarcastic, but it did not come out that way.

"There is another way," Inez said.

"What is that?" This is going too far, Karyn thought. I must stop humoring her.

"The bite of a werewolf, if it does not kill, can infect the victim with the taint. These cases are rare, because when a werewolf attacks, he usually kills. A blessing, in a way."

"I need a drink," Karyn said. "Do you want some more wine?"

"No, thank you."

Karyn went into the kitchen and made herself a strong Scotch and water. The way Inez was talking worried her, but she did not know how to ease away from the subject. She took a deep swallow of the drink before going back out.

"I can see I'm upsetting you," Inez said when Karyn came into the room.

"I'm sorry, Inez. I'm trying to listen seriously to what you're saying. But *werewolves*."

"Why is it so hard to accept? Don't we travel to the moon? Destroy cities with the force of the atom? Transplant organs from one human being to another?"

"But those are achievements of science. What you're talking about is superstition."

Inez's expression of utter conviction did not change.

Karyn took another approach. "All right, just for now let's say that these things do exist. Why here? Why in the Tehachapi Mountains of California? Why Drago?"

"The history of the town, for one thing," said Inez. "In the sixty-plus years that Drago has been in existence there have been an unreasonable number of strange deaths and unexplained disappearances in and around the village. I have books at home. Documents, records, newspaper clippings. I would have brought them with me tonight, but I didn't know you. I didn't know if I should bring up the subject."

"You still don't know me, Inez. I don't believe in your werewolves or your Devil or your God, and I don't want to hear any more about them." Karyn stopped abruptly as she heard herself turning shrill.

Inez looked as though she had been slapped. "I'm sorry, Karyn. Please believe that I'm sorry. I had given up talking to people about this because I knew they would think I was crazy. As I told you, they already think I'm odd. I can just imagine their reaction if I told them there is a werewolf at large in Drago. I took a chance on telling you because I sensed a sympathetic feeling between us. The last thing I wanted to do was upset you."

"Shall we drop it?" Karyn said. "I don't want to talk about it any more." She placed her empty glass firmly on the table.

"I understand." Inez looked around uncertainly. "Well . . . I should be going."

Karyn walked with her to the door. "Inez, I didn't mean to snap at you. My nerves haven't been in the best shape lately. Please don't take it personally."

The taller woman touched her hand. "Really, it's all right. Goodbye, Karyn."

Karyn stood at the door watching Inez Polk walk to her car and drive away. Then she turned back and saw the books Inez had brought her from the library. For some reason she felt like crying.

CHAPTER NINE

~~~~~~

As Roy Beatty approached the village of Drago, he breathed deeply of the balsam-scented air. He was relieved to be away from Karyn and her hangups, even for a little while. And because he felt relieved, he was twisted by guilt. Karyn was his wife. Now, when she was having problems, was no time for him to be making up excuses to go to Los Angeles, or to be rushing out of the house the minute somebody else showed up to take over the burden of keeping her company.

The fact that he could not get to the pulse of his feelings disturbed him. Roy Beatty had always been in control of his life. He was not a complicated man. He did not like surprises, and he did not like conflicts. For most of his twenty-nine years Roy had managed to keep his life running as smoothly as an engineering project.

And that was the way his life had gone—neatly plotted

and well within tolerances—until that terrible afternoon when the shaky voice of his best friend on the telephone had brought him rushing home.

Now, just as he had begun to hope that the peace and quiet of Drago might help restore the Karyn he had loved, this business of the missing dog and the howling in the night had upset her again. When, Roy wondered bitterly, would life return to normal?

He came to the main street of Drago and turned to his right before really thinking about his destination. He had not intended to walk all the way to the village, but he had just kept walking. The logical thing to do now, he told himself, was to turn around and start back. However, a curious sense of excitement compelled him to continue down the street. When at last he came to a stop Roy had to admit this was where he had been coming all along. It was the little shop run by Marcia Lura.

He hesitated for a moment before opening the door. A kind of unnatural stillness hung over the town. He reminded himself that he was doing nothing wrong. Why should he not come to this shop? He might just find a nice little gift inside to take home to Karyn.

No, that would not do. The idea of the gift had just popped into his head, and he could not pretend to himself that it was the reason he had come. He was here because he wanted very much to see again the dark-haired woman.

He walked inside to the sound of the tinkling bell. Marcia Lura was standing in the center of the shop wearing a peasant blouse and a full, flowered skirt. She was looking at him.

"Hello," she said. "I expected you sooner."

"You knew I would come?"

"Of course. When you were in the other day I felt the attraction between us as strongly as you did. Are you going to tell me I'm wrong?"

Roy caught his breath. In the dim light of the shop

Marcia looked criminally beautiful. Her eyes seemed to have a light of their own. An intense pale green.

"No," he said. "You are not wrong."

"Are you uncomfortable with me?"

"A little. Believe it or not, I don't usually do things like this."

"I believe you," she said. Her smile showed strong white teeth. "And besides, you haven't really done anything yet."

Roy forced a laugh. It did not come out as casual as he intended. "What I had in mind was some sort of gift for my . . . my wife."

"Ah, yes. Do you see anything you like?" Marcia's mouth curled faintly at the corners. Her eyes challenged him. "What I mean, of course, is anything your wife would like."

Roy looked around in confusion. His hand closed mindlessly on the nearest object, a china figurine of a little girl in the costume of a shepherdess. It was overly cute with blue saucer eyes and round cherub cheeks. Karyn would hate it.

"How much is this?" he said.

"Is that what you really want?"

"Why not?"

"It is seven dollars."

"I'll take it."

Marcia moved toward him, stopping just before they touched.

"Do you want to go for a walk with me?" she said.

"Walk?" Roy had to clear his throat against the sudden huskiness of his voice. "Walk where?"

"Out in the back. There's a path through the woods. It's very pretty this time of year."

"All right," he said, nodding.

"Come this way." She held aside the curtain at the rear of the shop. Beyond it were a small living room, kitchenette, bedroom, and bath. The rugs and the furni-

ture were in muted earth colors of brown, green, and
burnt orange. There were cushions on the floor and
candles everywhere. The air held a hint of sandalwood.

Marcia led him through her small apartment and out
the back door. There the forest pushed almost up to the
rear wall of the building, as it did to all buildings in
Drago. A broad path carpeted with pine needles led off
among the trees.

"Come." Marcia held out her hand to him. The fingers
were slim and white and well shaped. Roy took the hand.
The effect of the touch was like the spreading warmth
from the first sip of a good martini.

Hand in hand they walked along the path through the
forest. The shadows were deepening, and the afternoon
was cool. Occasionally Marcia would call his attention
to an unusual flower or a bird watching them from a tree.
Roy would respond to whatever she said, but his thoughts
were far from his words. He was acutely aware of the
waves of sensation that pulsed through his body from
the point where their hands touched. The green of her
eyes, he saw, was darker here in the forest. Deeper. The
loose black hair framed her face like softly folded wings.

"Strangely enough," Marcia was saying, "this path
leads through the woods and comes out on the road by
the old Fenno house." She turned the green eyes full
upon him. "I should really say the Beatty house now,
shouldn't I?"

"That has a permanent sound to it," Roy said. "We
only leased the place for six months."

"Really?"

"That was the plan. It's always possible we might
stay longer." He pulled himself away from the compelling
eyes, forced his thoughts down another channel. "Speaking of the Fennos, how well did you know them?"

"I hardly ever saw them," Marcia said. "They were
quite old, and seldom left the house."

"What happened to them, anyway?"

"I really couldn't say." Her manner chilled markedly. "I had no interest in them."

Suddenly Roy did not give a damn about the Fennos or their fate or anything at all except the woman before him. He gripped her hand and pulled her close, feeling the surprising strength in her arm as he did so.

"Marcia, I don't want to talk about the Fennos."

She looked into his eyes. She was a tall woman and could meet him almost on a level. "I know what you want, Roy. That's what I want too."

He started to speak, but she placed two fingers on his lips to silence him.

"Not yet," she said.

"Why?" he asked in a hoarse whisper. He felt like a preadolescent trying for a first kiss.

"It's not the right time."

"When?"

"You will know." Abruptly her mood changed and the contact was broken. "Come, let's go back."

They walked back along the path toward the village. Marcia danced on ahead, humming a melody Roy did not know. He followed along behind, feeling his desire for her flow powerfully through his veins. Still, he knew somehow that she was right. This was not the time. And he knew sure as death that the time would come.

They reached Marcia's shop at the edge of the forest and went in through the back door. They crossed the living quarters and went past the curtain into the front of the shop.

"It's been awfully nice," Marcia said. "We must do it again." The playful half-smile and the spark in her eyes said the things her words did not.

"Goodbye," said Roy. He started toward the door, his eyes still on Marcia.

"Aren't you forgetting something?"

"Am I?"

"The gift for your wife."

"Yes, I almost did forget. The little shepherdess. How much did you say it was?"

"Seven dollars."

Roy pulled a five and two ones from his wallet and handed the bills to her.

"Would you like a gift box?"

"No, thanks. I'll just take it as is."

Marcia slipped the china figurine into a plain paper sack and handed it to Roy. He took the package from her, turned quickly, and walked out. It was a gift, he realized, he would never deliver.

Back out on the street he thought, *This is crazy. No woman has had an effect like that on me since I was sixteen years old.*

It was the mountain air, he told himself. Plus the undeniable fact that Marcia Lura was a damned sexy woman. Even so, if sex were better for him and Karyn, it would never have happened.

But, damn it, nothing *had* happened. He had held a woman's hand, gone for a walk, and got an erection. Why did he feel as though he had cruelly betrayed his wife? There had not been even a mention of sex. Not aloud. Not in so many words. Nevertheless, as his house came into view, Roy had to admit that the short walk through the woods with Marcia had been an erotic experience he would not soon forget.

CHAPTER
TEN

"I'm sorry, Oriole, I'm just not with it today," Karyn said.

This was the third day in a row she had come in to the store and sat playing gin with Oriole. Roy had so immersed himself in his technical reports he was hardly stimulating company. He had urged her to amuse herself.

"You can say that again," Oriole replied. "You want some more coffee? A piece of pie? I made some fresh pumpkin."

Karyn looked at her wrist watch. "Gosh, no, look what time it is. I've got to get home and start dinner. Roy is having problems with his work, and I don't want to add to them by making him eat late."

"I'd give you a ride," Oriole said, "but Etienne took the pickup over to Palmdale for supplies."

Karyn walked to the back window and peered out into

the gathering darkness. "I'll make it all right, but I'd better get moving."

"There's a shortcut that will save you ten minutes. It comes out on the road not far from your place, if you don't mind walking through the woods."

"No, why should I? Where is this shortcut?"

"It's a nice wide path, easy to follow, starts right behind Marcia Lura's place. You know where that is?"

"Yes, I know."

"I can walk over there with you."

"Thanks, Oriole, I'll find it."

Karyn left the store and walked up the street to Marcia Lura's shop. As usual, the curtain was drawn over the front window, and there was no sign of life inside. A narrow passageway led back between the shop and the boarded-up building next door. Marcia's living quarters were dark too. What did the woman do in there, Karyn wondered. Probably sat with the lights out burning incense and chanting spells. Now where had that thought come from? Enough.

The path through the woods was, as Oriole had said, wide and easy to follow. However, the overhead branches blocked out much of the sky. The night seemed to follow just a few yards behind Karyn.

Someone called her name. Karyn stopped abruptly. A whisper more than a call, but distinct over the other rustlings of the forest. Karyn peered through the heavy brush that grew along the side of the path. At first she saw nothing, then there was a movement. A person. Man or woman, Karyn could not tell, but somebody was there, just a few yards away.

"Who's there? Who is it?"

No response.

Could it be Roy playing some kind of trick on her? No, he would never do that. Oriole Jolivet come to tell her she had forgotten something? But why would Oriole slip through the brush instead of following on the path? Why would anyone?

For an instant panic seized her, and Karyn's impulse was to run blindly for home. She fought it down. The nonsense talked by Inez Polk the other night must have unsettled her more than she realized. If she started running from shadows now, she would really be in trouble.

It was still not quite dark. Karyn parted the brush and took one cautious step off the trail. Then another. She would go just far enough to see what had attracted her eye. It would be some oddly shaped clump of brush, or a fallen branch that would look, when quickly seen, like somebody out there. The illusion, coupled with the call of an unfamiliar bird, would make it seem someone had called out to her.

Beneath the tang of evergreen there was another smell here. Something unpleasant and vaguely familiar. Something on the ground, partly hidden by the undergrowth, caught her eye. Something red with a bit of metal attached. Karyn reached down and grasped the red thing. Her hand came away holding the red leather collar, still buckled. Still on the ground was the head of the dog.

Karyn stiffened in shock. Her breath seemed suspended. A little way beyond where she stood, at the spot where she had thought she'd seen someone, there was no one now. Still, something was here. Something watching her. Something Evil.

Karyn's breath returned in a great ragged gasp. She staggered back onto the path and began to run. She ran blindly, her feet pounding the carpet of needles that covered the trail. Branches seemed to whip out and clutch at her. Behind her, moving silently through the trees, something followed.

When she reached the house Karyn could not make her fingers work to get the door open. She balled her hands into fists and pounded frantically on the panel.

When the door opened suddenly she half fell into the room.

Roy moved quickly to catch her. "Karyn! My God, what's the matter?"

Words would not come right away. "L-let me get my breath." Karyn allowed herself to be led to a chair. She sat down and fought for composure, knowing that in her breathless, disheveled state she must look like a mad woman.

Roy held her hand, rubbing it absently as he looked into her eyes. "Are you hurt?"

She shook her head, then pulled in a deep, slow breath. "Roy, I found Lady. I mean I found all that was left of her."

"You found her?" Roy repeated, his eyes searching her face.

Karyn raised her free hand, the one clutching the red leather collar with the buckle still fastened. "Out in the woods, alongside the path between here and Drago. I saw something in the brush and went over to look. Roy, it was her head. Just her head." Karyn broke off as she heard her voice begin to rise, and tried to will herself to be calm.

Roy took the collar from her and held it gingerly. "Poor Karyn, that must have been awful for you."

Karyn chewed her lip, wanting to tell him the rest, but wanting to sound in control.

"It looks like Anton Gadak was right," Roy said. "Some damned coyote got her. It's a rotten shame."

Karyn shook her head from side to side. "No."

"What do you mean?"

"It was something else. I . . . I think it followed me."

"Followed you *home*?"

She nodded.

Roy spun away from her and strode to the door. He pulled it open and stepped outside. After a minute he came back in. "There's no sign of anything out there.

What was it you thought you saw?"

"I'm not sure. Somebody . . . an animal . . . something."

She saw his face change. The look of deep concern faded into one of doubt.

"Why don't you go in and lie down, Karyn? I'll make you a hot toddy."

She leaped to her feet and faced him. "I don't want to lie down. And I don't want a goddam hot toddy. Something is out there, Roy. It followed me home through the woods."

"We'll go out and have a look in the morning," he said in a voice meant to be soothing. "Things never seem so frightening in the daylight."

"Damn you, Roy, don't patronize me!" Unable to stop herself, Karyn flailed at Roy's chest with her fists. "I'm not a child! I'm not hysterical!" Even as the words came out Karyn realized how childish and hysterical they sounded. Her body shook uncontrollably and she began to cry.

Roy wrapped his arms around her, and it felt good to be held.

"I'll put you to bed," he said. "Then I'm going for a doctor."

Karyn tried to speak, but great wracking sobs made it impossible. Roy led her into the bedroom and helped remove her clothes. He laid her gently in the big bed and tucked the blankets in around her.

"Will you be all right?" he said. "I'll lock the door."

"Roy, I'm not sick."

"Hush. You stay here and rest."

Before Karyn could protest, he hurried out of the house, started the car, and drove off toward Drago.

Oriole Jolivet was sitting behind the counter working a jigsaw puzzle when Roy entered the store. Etienne was washing down the meat case.

"Well, Roy," Oriole began, "we haven't seen you in

a month of Sundays. Karyn was just—"

Roy cut her off. "I need a doctor, Oriole. Is there one in town?"

The stout woman's face sobered. "What's the matter? Did something happen to Karyn?"

"She found the . . . the remains of our little dog in the woods. The shock hit her kind of hard."

"I bet it did, the poor kid. I was saying she just left here not an hour ago. Bill Volkmann's probably home now. He's the only doctor we got, but he's a good one."

"Can you tell me where to find him?"

"I can do better than that." Oriole came around to the front of the counter, laying aside her apron. "I'll ride along and show you." She looked over at her husband, who was watching them silently. "I'll be back directly."

Etienne Jolivet nodded gravely. Roy and Oriole hurried out to the car.

The house Oriole directed him to was on one of the short side streets between the Jolivets' store and the road that led to Roy and Karyn's house. It was an old two-story frame building painted an uninspired brown. The lawn was well kept and the shrubbery trimmed. There were no flowers.

"Bill Volkmann has lived here alone ever since his wife died in '71," Oriole said. "A couple times a week he'll go over to Pinyon to help out in the hospital there, but mostly he's retired now."

They climbed the steps to the front porch and Oriole twisted the key of an old-fashioned doorbell set into the heavy oak door.

The man who opened it was tall and lean, with a narrow, aristocratic face and steel-gray hair combed back from a high forehead. He wore a suit and vest that was of good quality though at least twenty years behind current styles.

"Bill, this is Roy Beatty," Oriole said. "The one moved

into the old Fenno place. His wife is down sick and he wanted a doctor."

"How do you do," said Dr. Volkmann in a deep, resonant voice. "I'm sorry to hear Mrs. Beatty is ill. What seems to be the trouble?"

"I think it's her nerves mostly," Roy said. "Karyn hasn't been really well for a couple of months, and this evening she had a scare while she was walking in the woods. When she got home she was shaking and not making a lot of sense, so I put her to bed and came looking for a doctor."

"Sounds like you did the right thing, but I'll be glad to come out and see her if you like."

"I'd appreciate it."

The doctor picked up his bag, an old-style black satchel, from a hall table and went out with Roy and Oriole to the car. They had little to say during the short drive to the house.

Karyn was sitting in the living room when they arrived. She was wearing a robe and had the quilt from the bed wrapped around her. She nodded a hello to Oriole.

"Karyn, this is Dr. Volkmann," Roy said.

She smiled at him briefly. "I hope you didn't leave anything important to come out here, Doctor. I'm really not sick."

"Well, you don't look sick," Volkmann said. "And you're taking me away from nothing but a lonely house and a dull book."

The doctor's deep voice and his dark, sensitive eyes were reassuring. Karyn relaxed a little.

"As long as I'm here, I might as well have a look at you," he said.

"It couldn't hurt, I guess," Karyn said. She led the way into the bedroom and sat on the edge of the bed while Dr. Volkmann took her temperature and blood pressure, counted her pulse, and talked quietly about nothing in particular. Roy remained in the living room with Oriole.

Volkmann smiled at her. "Well, young lady, there doesn't seem to be anything seriously wrong."

"I didn't think there would be," she said, "but it's always reassuring to hear it from a doctor. The whole thing was a case of nerves brought on by something that happened today."

"Your husband told me what happened." Volkmann fished in his bag and brought out two small pill bottles. "One of these is a mild sedative and the other a tranquilizer. I want you to take one of the little white pills after meals and one of the pink capsules before going to bed at night. Will you do that?"

Karyn repeated the instructions.

"Good." Volkmann went into the bathroom and came back with a glass of water. He shook one of the pink capsules from the bottle into her hand. "Take this now, and you should get a good night's sleep."

Karyn swallowed the capsule with water.

"If you run out of the medication, come and see me," Volkmann said. "However, I think you'll be feeling much better by that time. Much better, more relaxed, no problems."

"Thank you, Doctor," Karyn said. She sighed deeply, then returned his smile.

"My house is the brown one on the first road this side of the Jolivets' store. Drop in any time."

"I may do that," Karyn said.

"Goodnight, Mrs. Beatty." Dr. Volkmann snapped off the light and went back into the living room. He left the door slightly ajar.

Roy broke off his conversation and turned to the doctor. "How is she?"

"A slight nervous condition," Volkmann said, "aggravated by her experience in the forest today. I left her some mild medication. The best thing now is rest and quiet and living a normal life."

"Would it help if I took her away from Drago?" Roy asked.

Volkmann pursed his lips. "I don't think so. It would only make your wife feel she's being treated like an invalid. This is probably as good a place for her as any."

"Then there's nothing . . . seriously wrong with Karyn?"

"Not that I could determine from a very superficial examination. If there are problems, bring her in to see me. I don't think there will be."

"Thank you, Doctor. It was good of you to come out."

"Not at all. I enjoy meeting any new people in the community. We get so few."

"So I understand."

Volkmann shook his head sadly. "Yes, like so many small towns, I fear Drago is dying."

Oriole spoke up. "Bill Volkmann, if you start talking all gloomy like that you'll talk Roy and Karyn right out of Drago."

The doctor gave a soft laugh. "As long as we have people with your spirit, Oriole, the town will be all right."

"How much do I owe you, Doctor?" Roy said.

"Let me see . . . twenty-five dollars will cover it, but there's no hurry."

Roy went to the desk and pulled out a checkbook. "I come from a family of compulsive bill payers, so I'd just as soon keep us even from the start."

Volkmann smiled. "It would be foolish of me to argue with that."

After Roy had driven the doctor and Oriole back to town he hurried home to find Karyn sleeping peacefully. Her breathing was deep and regular, her color good. Roy leaned down and kissed her cheek softly, relieved.

A few minutes later he was very glad that she was asleep. Because in sleep she could not hear what he heard off somewhere in the night. The howling.

CHAPTER ELEVEN

~~~~~~

The pills that Dr. Volkmann left did wonders for Karyn's nerves over the next two days. The grisly discovery in the woods seemed little more than a bad dream now.

Roy stayed close to her and was very attentive. Karyn kept telling him she was really all right, but she could see in his eyes that he was not convinced.

On the second day Roy drove over to Pinyon and came back with a shotgun.

"What's that for?" Karyn asked.

"It's a confidence builder," Roy said. "So you'll know you have a weapon in the house when I'm not here."

"But I've never fired a gun in my life."

"This one's very simple to operate. I can show you how in a few minutes."

They went out to a clearing in the woods and Roy set

up a cardboard box for a target. He paced off twenty feet.

"No point in worrying about hitting anything farther away than this," he said.

The gun was a lightweight, single-barrel, 12-gauge model. Roy showed Karyn how to hold it and load it and finally how to pull back the hammer and fire. The first time it jolted her shoulder and the shot spattered up into the trees. Roy had her change her stance, and after that it was not so bad.

It took several more shots before she learned not to flinch when the gun went off, and even then she was still hitting the dirt a foot or so to the right of the box.

"You're jerking the barrel over when you pull the trigger," Roy said. "Squeeze it gently."

To Karyn the whole business seemed foolish, but if Roy had gone to all the trouble of getting the gun for her, the least she could do was go along with him. She followed his directions and soon was hitting the target.

The next day Roy drove into Drago for the mail and came back muttering to himself.

"Something the matter?" Karyn asked.

"They've got trouble at the office. Somebody turned up a bunch of errors in a set of weapons-system books we did, and there's a man from the Department of Defense coming in this afternoon for explanations."

"Will you have to be there?"

"I'm afraid so. It will probably be a late session tonight, and I may have to go back in tomorrow."

"It would be silly for you to drive all the way back here," Karyn said. "Why don't you stay overnight in Los Angeles and come home tomorrow when you've finished?"

"You're sure you'll be all right?"

"I'm sure. Anyway, I have your blunderbuss to deal with anything that goes bump in the night."

After several more assurances from Karyn, Roy

gathered his things quickly and drove off for the city.

With Roy gone, Karyn suddenly felt the emptiness and the isolation of the house. Although she was already ahead of schedule, she went to the bathroom and took another of Dr. Volkmann's tranquilizers.

About noon there was a knock on the door. Karyn opened it and found a young couple standing outside. They were dressed in hiking clothes. The boy carried a backpack and had one arm around the girl, supporting her.

"I wonder if we could use your phone?" the boy said. "My friend's had a fall and hurt her ankle."

"We left our van parked down in the village," the girl said.

"I'm sorry," Karyn said, "I don't have a phone. My car isn't here either, so I can't offer you a ride in. How bad is the ankle?"

"It's just a slight sprain from the looks of it," the boy said, "but it's too painful to walk on unless it's wrapped up."

"I lost the first-aid kit with my pack when I fell," the girl said. "We probably should have stayed on the easy trail up the mountain, but I wanted to try the hard way."

"Come inside," Karyn said. "I have some bandages and things."

"We'd appreciate it," the boy said. "This one doesn't look very heavy, but I don't think I could carry her much farther."

The girl made a face at him as he lifted her gently and carried her inside to the sofa.

The young couple introduced themselves as Neal Edwards and Pam Sealander. They lived together in Santa Barbara and often went backpacking in these mountains. They were a bright, attractive pair, and Karyn felt refreshed by their company.

Karyn found a package of Epsom salts with the medical supplies, and prepared a solution in a deep basin.

"Soak your foot in this," she told Pam, "and the swelling is supposed to go down. Don't ask me why, but it works."

Meanwhile Neal went outside and came back with a stout forked branch. He used a hatchet to shape it into a serviceable crutch.

"Now we're all set," Neal said. "As soon as the swelling goes down we can tape up the ankle and Pam should be able to walk all right with the crutch."

"There's no hurry, is there?" Karyn said. "I'm glad to have some company. Why don't I make some sandwiches?"

"We sure wouldn't turn them down," Neal said, grinning.

Karyn prepared a tray of sandwiches and a pot of coffee. The three of them sat together at the table eating and enjoying the cool afternoon.

"It's lucky for us somebody was living here," Pam said. "This house has been empty for years."

"Yes, I know," Karyn said. "My husband and I just took a six-month lease on the place."

"I didn't think you looked like regular Drago people," Neal said.

"Oh? Why not?"

"It's hard to say exactly. They're . . . different. I guess part of it is living in this isolated valley out of the mainstream. And maybe it's a heritage they bring from the old country."

"Old country?"

"I just meant that most of the people in Drago seem to be from the same European background. They're sort of a closed society."

"Some of them seem quite friendly," Karyn said.

"I'm sure they are once you get to know them," Pam said. "A lot of people are prejudiced because of the stories."

"What stories?" Karyn had an uncomfortable feeling

she had been in this conversation before.

"Just a lot of tall tales," Neal said. "The kind of thing kids make up around a campfire. Nothing you'd take seriously."

"Maybe *you* wouldn't," Pam said, "but I'd give it a lot of thought before I came into this valley alone. They say people disappear here without a trace."

"Sure, it's the Haunted Forest," Neal said, laughing. He put an arm around the girl's shoulder. "Anyway, you've got big strong me along for protection."

Pam laughed with him. "I'm so lucky."

Karyn was relieved that the conversation had turned away from things she did not want to hear. She excused herself for a moment and took another tranquilizer. She forgot what it was that had disturbed her. It didn't matter.

The rest of the afternoon passed quickly. The young couple told Karyn about their life in Santa Barbara, and she told them about growing up in New York and how different it was in California. Before anyone realized it the sun was gone and the mountain shadows had reached into the valley.

Neal looked out the window, then checked his watch. "It's getting late. How's the ankle, Pam?"

The girl got to her feet and took a few steps with the the makeshift crutch. "It feels a lot better. I can make it all right if we go slowly."

"You're welcome to spend the night here," Karyn said. "There's an extra bedroom."

"Thanks," Neal said, "but we really should be getting back. There's a path through the woods not far from here that will take us into town faster than your road."

"Yes, I know the path," Karyn said.

Neal wrapped Pam's foot and ankle tightly with adhesive tape, and they said goodbye to Karyn, telling her to look them up if she came to Santa Barbara. With Neal's powerful flashlight showing the way, they moved off toward the path. Karyn watched until the light disappeared among the trees. Then she bolted the door, took a sleeping pill, and began to prepare for bed.

Neal and Pam were about halfway to the village when Pam stopped suddenly. Resting on her makeshift crutch, she put a hand on the boy's arm.

"What is it?" he said.

"I thought I heard something. Out there."

"Heard what?"

"Listen."

Silence for a moment, then a sharp rustling of the brush as something moved toward them. Something big. Neal beamed the flashlight into the darkness toward the sound.

It came at them fast, bright-orange eyes reflecting the light.

"Neal, what is it?" Pam cried.

Instinctively, Neal placed himself in front of the girl. "I don't know."

Heedless of the heavy undergrowth, the beast crashed toward them. From ten feet away it sprang, and for an instant seemed to hang in the air—thick fur bristling, muscles tensed, black lips drawn back along the muzzle showing vicious yellow teeth.

"My god!" Neal gasped, and the beast was on him. It hit him high on the chest, the forepaws bearing him to the ground. The boy had time for one terrible scream before the teeth tore into his windpipe.

The flashlight rolled crazily along the path, throwing leaping shadows among the trees. Pam, her mouth open and dry with terror, used her crutch to club at the dark snarling form that crouched over Neal's body. The jaws worked and there was a sickening crunch of bone.

Again and again Pam struck at the animal without effect. At last the crutch broke in her hands and the beast raised its head and looked at her. The muzzle was dark and dripping.

"No! Oh, no!" the girl screamed. She turned to run, but the ankle gave way and she stumbled and fell forward. The animal landed on her back, blasting the air from her lungs. Her last sensation was the powerful jaws clamping onto the base of her skull.

CHAPTER TWELVE

~~~~~~

Karyn awoke slowly, reluctantly, from the drugged sleep. Outside the morning was bright and fresh, but to Karyn the world seemed to exist on the far side of a gray scrim curtain. Her mouth was stale. It was an effort to move her limbs.

She put an arm over to touch Roy, but his side of the bed was empty. It was several minutes before her sluggish mind recalled that Roy had spent the night in the city. It would have been sweet just to lie there in bed thinking about nothing. Pull the comforter up over her head and shut out the morning. Karyn sighed. She really ought to get up, she told herself.

Getting out of bed was so much work that she had to sit on the edge for a minute and rest. At last she stood up and went to the closet. She pulled on an old bathrobe of Roy's. It was too much bother to think about a shower or brushing out her hair.

She went into the kitchen, but fixing breakfast held no appeal. There were dishes unwashed from the day before, but they could wait. She walked into the livingroom and sat in the chair by the window and looked down at her hands.

She was still sitting in the chair at eleven-thirty when a car pulled up outside. Footsteps crunched across the drying grass in the clearing. Someone knocked at the door. With a heavy sigh Karyn rose from the chair and walked over to see who it was.

Chris Halloran stood in the doorway looking casual and fresh in checked slacks and a brown pullover sweater. The smile of greeting he had ready stiffened when he took a look at Karyn.

"Why, Chris, what a surprise."

It took him a second to answer. "Hello, Karyn. I had a couple of days off, so I thought I'd drive out and see how you guys are doing."

"That's nice."

He waited for her to say something else. When she didn't, he said, "Is it all right if I come in?"

Karyn put on a smile. It felt lopsided. "Yes, of course, please come in, Chris. I'm a little slow this morning."

Chris came into the room, keeping his eyes on Karyn. "Where's Roy?"

"He went into the city. It seems he has to spend more time in Los Angeles than he thought he would. Isn't that interesting?"

"Karyn, are you all right?"

"Why? Is something the matter?"

"You look a little . . . tired."

Karyn looked down at the old robe she was wearing and put a hand up to touch her unbrushed hair. "Oh, you mean this. I hadn't gotten around to getting dressed yet. What time is it, anyway?"

"Almost noon."

"Really? I must have dozed off in the chair."

"I should have let you know I was coming, but I didn't decide myself until this morning."

"No, that's all right. I'm always glad to see you. Can I get you anything?"

"I'm fine, Karyn. Sit down, please."

"I think I will, if you don't mind." She returned to the chair by the window and eased into it. It was true that she was glad to see Chris, but keeping the conversation going was an effort.

Chris perched uncomfortably on the edge of the sofa. "So tell me what's been happening."

"Not very much. It's a quiet life up here. We lost Lady."

"Lost her? What happened?"

Karyn looked out the window, her face empty of expression. "Something caught her in the woods and killed her."

Chris leaned forward, staring at her. "What are you talking about? *What* caught her?"

Karyn shrugged her shoulders. She felt loose and disjointed wearing the oversized robe. "I don't know what it was. The sheriff—but he's not really a sheriff—says it was a coyote. Or maybe it was an owl." She giggled suddenly and put a hand over her mouth like a little girl caught laughing in class.

Chris got up and walked over to her chair. He looked down into her face. "Karyn, what is the matter? I told you you look tired, but you don't. You look sick."

"I'm all right. I have some pills that I take for my nerves and to help me sleep. I'm all right."

"What kind of pills?"

"Who knows? Dr. Volkmann gave them to me."

"Who is Dr. Volkmann?"

"He's just Dr. Volkmann. He lives in Drago. He came out when I was sick."

"I don't know what he's giving you, but it doesn't look like it's helping a lot."

"Is that a comment on the way I look?"

"Karyn, I'm serious. We've been friends long enough so that I shouldn't have to play games. I think you should have another doctor examine you."

"Dr. Volkmann is a good doctor."

Chris started to say something more, then seemed to think better of it. "I'm sorry I missed Roy. We must have passed each other on the freeway."

"I don't think so. Roy drove in yesterday."

"And left you here alone?"

"It didn't matter. I had a nice young couple for company."

"Overnight?"

"No, they had to leave."

Chris shook his head slowly, but said nothing. He made several more attempts to kindle a conversation, but Karyn found it hard to concentrate on his words. She felt one step removed from everything that was happening. In a way it was a comfortable feeling, but in the depths of her consciousness she knew something was very wrong.

After a while they ran out of words and Chris moved toward the door. "I guess I might as well be heading back to L.A."

Karyn rose to walk out with him. She looked into his eyes and saw herself reflected in the pupils. There was something she would like to tell him, but it seemed too much trouble to put it into words. For some reason a tear formed in the corner of one eye and rolled down her cheek.

Chris took a step toward her. "You're not well. Let me take you to a doctor in Los Angeles."

She shook her head without saying anything. The tears came freely.

"Karyn, please, you've got to let me help you." He

reached out to her, grasping her shoulders, and pulled her against him.

Since the day she had been assaulted in the apartment no man but her husband had touched Karyn. Now, through some trick of the mind, she was back there. The gentle face of her friend Chris Halloran twisted and changed like a rubber mask into the foul leering thing that had attacked her. Chris's hands on her shoulders became the rough, grasping hands of the rapist. She pulled her head back to look into his face. He was saying something, but all she could see were his teeth. Teeth like those that had torn the flesh of her thigh and left her scarred down there.

"Get away from me!" she cried. "Get away! Don't touch me, you filthy animal!"

Instantly Chris pulled his hands away and stepped back, "Karyn, what's the matter with you? What are you saying?"

She balled her hand into a fist and swung at him. In his astonishment, Chris made no move to avoid the blow, and her fist smacked into the corner of his mouth, slicking his lip with blood.

He seized her wrists. "Have you gone crazy?"

"You'd better get out of here," she said, her voice rising hysterically. "If my husband finds you here he'll kill you."

Chris touched the corner of his mouth and looked at the blood on his fingertips. "All right, dammit, enough. I don't know what's happening to you up here, Karyn, but if this is the way you want it, it's your business. Excuse the intrusion."

He sidestepped her and shouldered out through the door. Karyn heard the car door slam. The engine roared to life and the Camaro spun away in an angry burst of gravel.

For several minutes she stood by the door, breathing raggedly, feeling her heart pound. The fog that had clouded her mind throughout the day had been shredded by Chris's sudden anger. She walked into the bathroom and ran the cold water. She caught it in her cupped hands and dashed it into her face. The cold shock helped to clear her head even more. She looked into the mirror and saw the pale, unkempt creature Chris had seen. What had come over her to act the way she had? For a terrible few seconds Chris had seemed to become the rapist. She had screamed at him, hit him, sent him away. What was happening to her?

CHAPTER THIRTEEN

~~~~~~

Karyn took a long steaming-hot shower, then forced herself to stand for twenty seconds while the water sprayed icy cold. She rubbed her body dry with a big rough towel and went out to the kitchen to start a pot of coffee. While it percolated she put on a clean pair of jeans and a light sweater. She drank the coffee black and strong, then brushed her teeth until her gums tingled. For the first time in days her body began to feel strong, her mind clear, with only traces of cobwebs. It was two o'clock when she left the house and walked briskly down the lane toward Drago.

By the time she had reached the blacktopped main street Karyn's legs ached from the unaccustomed activity after days of little exercise. Still, she felt refreshed and alert. The scent of the pines washed out her lungs as she swung down the drab street. Some movement down the street on the other side caught her eye, and she slowed her pace.

A tow truck was pulled up there in front of a metallic-blue van. The driver was out of the truck attaching a cable to the front of the van. Something stirred in Karyn's memory. She walked over to where the tow-truck driver stood between the two vehicles.

"Are you towing this van away?"

"That's right. You the owner?"

"No, but I think I know who is. Why are you taking it?"

"The Highway Patrol got an abandoned-vehicle report. When that happens we pull 'em in."

"Where did the report come from?"

The driver pulled a sheet of paper from his pocket and unfolded it. "Report phoned in by Anton Gadak. You know him?"

"I know him. Is he around?"

"He was here a few minutes ago to sign the towaway order. I think he went in the tavern up the street there."

Karyn hesitated for a moment. This was really none of her business. Yet in a way it was. She had liked young Neal Edwards and Pam Sealander. She thanked the tow-truck driver for the information and walked up the street toward the tavern where he had said Anton Gadak could be found.

It was dark inside. Most of the overhead bulbs were burned out, and the flickering beer signs behind the bar only deepened the shadows. The air was stale with old beer, the floor gritty beneath her feet. Karyn stood for a moment inside the door until her eyes adjusted to the gloom.

Anton Gadak sat midway along the bar with a glass of beer in front of him. On the next stool sat a paunchy man in overalls. They were the only customers. The bartender sat dozing in a wooden chair at the far end of the bar.

Karyn walked up behind Gadak and cleared her throat. "Excuse me."

The big man swiveled on his stool and looked at her. He touched the brim of his Stetson. "Afternoon, Mrs. Beatty."

"Can I talk to you for a minute?"

"Go ahead."

The man sitting next to Gadak got up and walked back to the men's room without looking at Karyn.

"What's on your mind?" said Gadak.

"There's a truck out in the street getting ready to tow away a van."

"That so?"

"The driver said you signed the order to have it towed away."

"Said that, did he?"

Sudden anger gave heat to Karyn's words. "Is there some reason you don't want to talk about it?"

Gadak's tolerant smile faded. "Suppose you tell me why you're so interested, Mrs. Beatty."

"I think I know the people who own the van."

"That's interesting. There was no registration slip in the thing. It was breakin' the law parked the way it was, so I had it towed away."

"Don't you want to know who the owner is?"

"Makes no difference to me. Somebody comes looking for it, I'll tell 'em where they can pick it up. It ain't my job to go find them."

Karyn held back a sharp retort. If Anton Gadak knew more than he was telling, and she felt sure he did, it would serve no purpose to anger the man.

"Thank you," she said coolly, and turned to walk out of the stale-smelling tavern. Outside the tow truck and the van were gone. Karyn crossed the street and went into the Jolivets' store.

Oriole greeted her enthusiastically. "Hey, Karyn, you're a sight for sore eyes. How you feeling?"

"Much better, Oriole. Thanks."

"Maybe we can get in a few hands of gin today. I tell you it's been mighty dull around here the last three days."

"I don't think I'm quite up to playing cards yet," Karyn said. "What I'd like is to use your phone, if it's all right."

"Help yourself. I'll be back in a minute."

When Oriole had gone out through the rear of the store to give Karyn privacy, Karyn riffled through the thin local phone book, praying that Inez Polk was listed. To her relief, the number was there. She picked up the phone and dialed.

Please be home, Inez. Please answer the phone.

"Hello?"

At the sound of Inez' voice Karyn wanted to cry out with joy. She willed herself to be calm.

"Inez, this is Karyn Beatty."

"Oh, yes, how are you, Karyn?"

Keeping her eye on the door leading to the back room, Karyn went on in a low tone. "Right now I'm not too good. I want to tell you first off that I'm terribly sorry for the way I acted the other night."

"Don't give it a thought. Your reaction was mild compared to some."

"Just the same, I was rude, and now I'm seeing things differently."

"Something has happened?"

"I don't want to go into it over the phone. Can you come to my place?"

"I have a meeting at the school here tonight, but if it's urgent I could miss it."

"It's not really that urgent, I guess."

"How about tomorrow?"

"That will be fine. And, Inez . . ."

"Yes?"

"Those books and things you told me about . . . would you bring them?"

"I'll bring them. Karyn, are you in any danger?"

"No, it's . . . I don't think so. I'll tell you about it tomorrow."

Karyn hung up the phone and started to turn. She jumped as she saw Etienne Jolivet standing a few feet away, watching her.

"Did I frighten you, Mrs. Beatty?" he said.

It was the first time Karyn had heard him speak. His voice was a monotone with a soft, unplaceable accent.

"I didn't see you standing there," she said.

Etienne smiled at her. A shallow smile that did not reach his eyes.

Oriole came back from the rear of the store. "Get your call made?"

"Yes, thanks."

"Sure you won't stay? Even for a cup of coffee?"

"No, I want to be home before dark. To be there when Roy gets back, I mean."

"Well, take it easy," Oriole said.

Karyn bought a pound of coffee just to be buying something, and left the store. She passed up Marcia Lura's shop, wanting nothing to do with the shortcut through the woods, and walked on down to where the narrow road turned off. All the way home she watched the brush on both sides as if expecting something unusual.

Once Karyn was inside the little house, the remainder of the afternoon seemed to drag interminably. She wished Roy would come home. She would tell him about the young hikers' van being towed away, and the strange guarded response of Anton Gadak when she asked about it. Maybe Roy would begin to see the strange things happening in Drago.

She prepared a simple cheese casserole so all she would have to do was pop it in the oven when Roy came home. After that she sat down to read, but found it difficult to concentrate. A very light Scotch and water calmed her as the sun slipped behind the western mountains and darkness spilled into the valley.

Then came the howling. Karyn leaped from the chair, dropping the book she was reading on the floor. This time it was right outside.

Karyn crossed the room in quick steps and pressed herself against the opposite wall. She stared at the front door, half expecting it to burst open.

Whatever was outside howled again—a wailing night cry that ended in an ominous growl. Karyn forced herself to walk back across the room to the front window. She parted the curtains and looked out. In the clearing in front of the house, less than twenty feet from the door, hunched a dark, sinister silhouette. Without taking her eyes from the window, Karyn reached over and fumbled along the wall for the switch to the outdoor light. She found it and flipped it on.

It was a wolf, but bigger than any wolf should be. As the animal sat on its haunches, the big head came to nearly four feet above the ground. It did not move when the light came on, but glared defiantly at the window. The reflected light of the bulb out in front made the eyes glow like jewels. The wolf's fur was a dull gray-brown color, shaggier around the neck. The chest was full, the large forepaws planted solidly on the ground. As Karyn watched, the thin black lips of the animal skinned back and she saw the teeth.

She fought down the terror that rose like bile in her throat. She would not live the rest of her life in fear. How dare this beast come to her house to intimidate her? Wolf, ghost, or werewolf—whatever it was, she would not yield to it without a fight. Letting the curtain fall back across the window, she went to the closet and took out the shotgun and the box of shells. She checked to be sure it was loaded.

She carried the gun and the box of shells back into the living room. That other time, back in the apartment in the city, she had been defenseless and overpowered when she was attacked. This time it would be different. She had a weapon.

Moving deliberately, Karyn unbolted the front door. She turned the knob and slowly, carefully pulled the door open.

The wolf rose with a rumbling growl. It began to move toward her.

The shooting lessons Roy had given her came back to Karyn in fragments. There was no time to try to remember everything. She shouldered the gun, aimed at the wolf, and pulled the trigger. The gun boomed and dirt exploded two feet to the right of the wolf. The animal stopped coming for a moment, but showed no fear.

Keeping a grip on her emotions, Karyn reloaded the gun, corrected her aim for the trigger pull, and fired again. The charge of shot hit the wolf full in the face. The animal made no sound, but the impact knocked it over backward. For a moment all four feet thrashed the air.

When the beast regained its footing one side of the massive head was raw and bleeding. However, the damage was far less than it should have been, considering the close-range shotgun blast. Karyn broke the weapon open and prepared to reload and fire again, but the wolf gave her no opportunity. It bounded away to the edge of the forest. There it stopped, looking back at her with raw animal hatred. After a moment it vanished among the trees.

Karyn went back into the house and leaned the shotgun against a wall. Breathing heavily, she sat down at the kitchen table to await Roy's arrival.

CHAPTER
FOURTEEN

Roy Beatty stopped in the doorway, a greeting frozen on his lips. In a glance he took in Karyn's controlled expression, her rigid posture in the chair, and the shotgun leaning against the wall.

"What happened?"

"It was here. The wolf. Right out in front of the house. I shot at it and hit it, but it got away."

Roy blinked, struggling to catch up. "A wolf?"

"Right outside. I shot it."

He walked over and looked down into Karyn's eyes. She looked frightened, but under control and rational enough. He went into the kitchen and found a flashlight in the tool drawer, then returned to Karyn.

"Show me where the animal was when you shot it."

Karyn got up and led him out the door and into the clearing in front of the house. Roy played the flashlight over the ground as they walked. Karyn stopped walking and pointed down at her feet.

"The wolf was right here," she said.

Roy knelt at the spot she indicated and slid the circle of light over the crisp dry grass. He reached down to touch a dark patch and held the light on his fingers. They were sticky with blood.

"I guess you really did hit something," he said.

"Not *something*, Roy. A wolf. The biggest wolf I've ever seen."

"All right, you shot a wolf. What happened next?"

"It ran off into the woods."

Roy swept the light over a larger area of ground. He spotted something a few feet away and went over to pick it up. It was a piece of ragged gray tissue the size of a playing card. He held it gingerly between thumb and forefinger.

Karyn came over to look. "What is it?"

"An ear."

Karyn turned away, shivering.

"You go on back in the house," he said. "I'll take a look around in the woods."

"Roy, don't go out there alone."

"I'll be careful. The shotgun's coming along too."

Karyn chewed her lip a moment before she spoke. "Roy, I don't think the shotgun can stop this wolf. I should have killed it with my shot, but it just came up bleeding a little."

"You probably didn't hit it as good as you think," Roy said. "If it's still around I'll finish it off."

They went inside and Roy took the shotgun from where Karyn had propped it against the wall. He put a fresh shell in the chamber and dropped several more into his jacket pocket.

"Keep the door locked while I'm gone," he said.

"Don't worry."

When Karyn had closed and locked the door behind

him, Roy walked to the edge of the clearing and swept the brush with the flashlight. He moved along slowly, examining the ground and the bushes. At one of the faint paths that led away from the house the light picked up something. Roy leaned down and saw a dime-sized spot of blood on a flat stone. Whatever it was that Karyn had shot must have come this way. Roy straightened and moved off along the path.

Overhead the high cloud layer began to break up, and a bright moon shone through the openings. Roy walked easily along the path with the shotgun in one hand and the flashlight beaming ahead of him.

A movement up ahead caught his eye and he stopped short.

He snapped off the light and stepped cautiously forward. In a small grassy clearing he saw it again—something pale caught in a flash of moonlight. Roy brought the shotgun to a ready position and waited, holding his breath.

"Are you going to stay there crouching in the bushes, or will you come and join me?" The woman's voice mocked him from the clearing.

Roy stepped toward the voice and snapped on the light. Marcia Lura looked back at him, her eyes glowing.

For a moment Roy could not move. Marcia wore a deeply cut gown in green and black, night colors of the forest. Her dark hair folded softly back over wide shoulders that gleamed palely in the light. There was no surprise in her face, just a faintly amused smile.

"My God, I almost shot you," Roy said.

"It's a strange time to be out hunting."

Roy lowered the flashlight beam from Marcia's face down over the lithe body. Its lines were clearly visible beneath the thin material of the gown. Suddenly uncomfortable, he snapped off the light.

"I was following a wounded animal. My wife shot at a wolf, she thinks, and it came this way."

"I saw no wolf," said Marcia, "or anything else."

"What are you doing out here, anyway?"

"I often walk in the forest at night. It's so very private."

"I suppose it would be."

"Have you ever tried it?"

"Not alone."

Roy found himself standing quite close to the tall supple woman. He was not sure whether he had walked across the clearing or she had come to him. It didn't matter. The scent of sandalwood clung to her. Sandalwood and something else . . . something wild.

"Would you like to walk with me?" she said.

The pale-green eyes caught the reflected moonlight and seemed to draw Roy down into them.

"Or would you rather do something else with me?"

With a swift, graceful movement Marcia unfastened the gown at her breast and let it slide down her body to make a dark pool at her feet. Beneath it she was naked. She stepped free of the fallen garment and moved back so he could see her.

Her body was lean and smooth, her breasts high. Her stomach was flat. Below the navel a wedge of silky black hair pointed to the joining of her legs.

"Do you like me?" she asked.

Roy could only answer honestly. "Yes." He realized he was still holding the flashlight and the gun. He let them drop.

"Come to me," Marcia said. She stood with her legs apart and held out her bare white arms to him.

Roy peeled off his clothes and tossed them aside. He felt the chill night air on his skin, and stepped forward quickly to take Marcia in his arms. The touch of her bare flesh was like a caress all up and down his body. She pressed herself against him. They kissed. Her mouth had the taste of wild berries. Desire for the woman overpowered his every civilized thought.

With Marcia Lura, Roy discovered a savage, abandoned

kind of sex, a kind he had never known. His body writhed and twisted in concert with hers. No inch of flesh, no orifice of the body went unexplored. Her long strong fingers were on him, in him. Her mouth swallowed him, her tongue darted and probed. He tasted her, he inhaled her, he groped for the essence of her.

The moon came and went as clouds pushed across the night sky. Time stopped. The climax, when it came, was sweet and wild and more complete than Roy hàd thought possible..They lay together afterward, their bodies cleaved into one. It was Marcia who made the first move. Gently she disengaged herself and sat up. She looked down at him, the curtain of black hair shading her face. The green eyes shone with a light of their own.

"God, you're beautiful," he said.

She reached down and placed her fingertips on his lips. He touched his tongue to her fingers and tasted the mingled juices of their bodies.

Marcia rose and moved silently to where her gown lay on the forest floor. She raised it over her head and let it slide down over her body. With her eyes on Roy, she fastened the garment over her breast.

"When will I see you?" he said.

"When you want me."

Before he could speak again Marcia stepped lightly out of the clearing and vanished among the dark trees. Roy pulled himself upright and found he was sore and exhausted and utterly drained. He moved awkwardly about, retrieving his scattered clothing.

When he was fully dressed again he let himself think about Karyn. She would be wondering why he was so long. Guilt gnawed like a parasite in his stomach.

Enough, he told himself. Feeling guilty would do no one any good. He had never claimed to be a saint. Marcia Lura had been there when he badly needed someone, and he had taken her. Or had she been the taker? It did not matter. The thing had happened, and he knew it would happen again. He picked up the gun and the flashlight and walked back along the path to the house.

Karyn was waiting for him at the door.

"I was getting worried." She stepped back and looked him over more carefully. "What happened to you?"

Roy looked down at his clothes, rumpled and speckled with dirt and pine needles.

"I thought I saw something and stumbled going after it. Turned out to be just a shadow."

"Oh?" One small syllable containing a world of female doubt.

"I didn't find a thing. As I said, whatever it was you shot at is long gone by now."

"Did you hurt yourself when you fell?"

"No, I'm just tired. Why don't we go to bed?"

"Do you want something to eat?"

"No, just a shower and bed."

Roy stepped around her and went into the bathroom. He undressed and got into the shower, where he lathered his body over and over to wash away the smell of the other woman. As he massaged his soapy skin the memory of Marcia's hands on him began to arouse him again. He turned the water on full cold and stood under it until his erection went down. He dried himself off, fell into bed, and was asleep in seconds. When Karyn got in beside him he did not stir. He was deep in a dream of the dark woods and the savage love of a green-eyed woman.

CHAPTER FIFTEEN

~~~~~~

Karyn stood gazing down at Roy as he slept. He had been so exhausted when he came in last night that she decided not to wake him. His sleep was restless. He wore a troubled frown, and his body twitched in rhythm to some vivid dream.

Karen only left him when Inez Polk arrived. Her arms were laden with books and folders that contained old newspaper clippings. Karyn met her at the door and helped carry the books inside and set them on the table. She turned then and took Inez' hands in her own.

"I'm glad you're here," she said. "So many things have happened."

Inez' long homely face broke into a smile. "I'm glad I'm here too. Now, let's sit down and you can tell me what's been going on."

Karyn poured out what remained of the coffee, and

they sat down at the table. Inez listened attentively as Karyn related the events of the past few days. She told of finding Lady's remains in the woods, and about the young backpackers who had spent the day with her, then walked away to an unknown fate. She described Anton Gadak's evasiveness when she asked about the van. Finally she told of the huge wolf that had sat outside the house last night, how she had fired at it and wounded it, and how Roy had gone looking for it afterward but found no trace.

"What's your feeling now?" Inez asked when Karyn had finished her story. "Are you ready to talk about a werewolf?"

Karyn took a moment before she replied. "I'm ready to accept the possibility, yes. Every logical bone in my body rejects the idea, but I can't forget the look of that . . . that thing in front of my house last night. It was much too big and too, well, malevolent to be a natural wolf. Altogether too many unexplained things have been happening. If you tell me there is a werewolf, I'll listen."

Inez arranged the books and papers neatly in front of her and adjusted her glasses. "The first thing we must be sure of is that we understand what we're dealing with. How much do you know about werewolves, Karyn?"

"Not an awful lot. They're something like vampires, aren't they?"

"Not at all," Inez said briskly. "The vampire is a dead creature that sustains a form of life by subsisting on human blood. A vampire may continue in this undead state for hundreds of years. The werewolf, on the other hand, is as much alive as you or me. Its lifespan is no greater than normal, and when once they die, they are dead forever. There are, of course, certain similarities. When he assumes the wolf form, the werewolf, like the vampire, has a strength far beyond normal, and ordinary weapons cannot destroy him."

"Is there no defense against them?" Karyn asked. "Garlic at the windows? A cross?"

"No, those are weapons against the vampire. Only two things can destroy the werewolf—one is fire, the other silver."

"Oh, yes, the silver bullet."

Inez permitted herself a thin smile. "I guess that's the one everybody knows."

"One thing here doesn't fit with what I've heard of werewolves. During the past weeks I've either heard or seen something almost every night. Aren't they supposed to come out only during the full moon?"

"Oh, no, they can change any night once the sun has gone down. But let me start at the beginning."

Speaking with quiet intensity, Inez related the history and the nature of werewolves. Frequently she referred to the stack of books she had brought. Among them were *The Book of Were-Wolves* by Sabine Baring-Gould, *Lycanthropy in London* by Dudley Costello, *The Cult of the Werewolf in Europe* by Lewis Spence, and *The Werewolf* by Montague Summers. There were books in French —*Le Loup-Garou de Provence;* German—*Volkssagen aus Pommern und Rugen;* and Latin—*Malleus Maleficarum.* And other books in languages Karyn did not recognize.

Inez showed Karyn passages dealing with cases of werewolfism over the years, some documented, some legendary. There was the notorious Peter Stubbe, tried and executed in 1590 for a series of bloody killings near Cologne while in the form of a wolf. There was the doomed crew of the Spanish vessel *Louisa* that met a ghastly fate on the Aegean island of Skiathos, said to be infested with werewolves. There was the lost Bulgarian village of Dradja where the cruelest torture by an avenging mob could not force the villagers to give up the killer beast that dwelt among them.

Most of the stories dated from the sixteenth and seventeenth centuries, but there were reports of werewolves as early as the writings of Herodotus in 450 B.C., and as recently as the New Orleans *Times-Picayune* in 1959.

"The local newspaper clippings you can go over yourself," Inez said. "The earliest I could find was in 1919. Altogether, there have been sixteen reported deaths or disappearances in this valley with no logical explanation. Your two young friends with the van would make eighteen."

"Still," Karyn said, "that's more than fifty years, and this is a wilderness area where a lot of things can happen to people."

"Those are only the *reported* cases. I know of at least two that never made the papers."

"Oh?"

"Has anyone told you what happened to the people who lived in this house before you?"

"The Fennos? No."

"It was just over four years ago. The old people hadn't been seen in town for a week or so, and there were inquiries. Your friend Anton Gadak came out to investigate. He found the two of them dead. Supposedly, natural causes."

"That's not so strange. The Fennos were quite old, weren't they?"

"There's more. About a week later one of my pupils, a little boy whom I've never known to lie, told me that he and a friend had sneaked into the house to look around. They found it all torn up, with dried blood everywhere, and bits of flesh and bone scattered about. The boys hadn't said anything at first for fear of getting into trouble."

"Did you report it?"

"I told the boy to tell his parents. He did, and they reported it to the county sheriff. The sheriff sent a couple of men out to look the house over, but they found nothing unusual. They put it down to the child's active imagination."

"But you don't think so," Karyn put in.

"No. I think somebody came in here after the boys saw it and cleaned up."

The women sat without speaking for several minutes. Finally Karyn said, "All right, what do we do now? Try to convince someone in authority that there's a werewolf loose in Drago?"

Inez smiled wryly. "What do you think our chances would be?"

"Pretty slim," Karyn admitted. "But there must be something we can do."

"Wait a minute, maybe there is." Inez was suddenly sitting on the edge of her chair. "You wounded the wolf last night?"

"That's right. I hit him—it—in the face with the shotgun. It tore off an ear, I think."

"Good. You see, when a werewolf is wounded, it can change back to human form, but it will have an identical injury. Their wounds heal unnaturally fast, but if you can find them soon enough it's a giveaway."

When Karyn looked doubtful, Inez referred again to her books. She quoted the story of a traveler through Wales who was attacked by a wolf, but managed to hack off one of the beast's paws and escape. The next morning he was horrified to see his landlady at the inn with fresh bandages covering the stump of her right hand. And the notorious Parenette Gandillon, after villagers with clubs had driven off a wolf, was found moaning in her bed covered with bruises.

"Assuming these old reports are accurate," Inez concluded, "what we must do is look for someone in Drago with a missing ear."

"And suppose we find him," Karyn said. "What then?"

Inez started to answer, but hesitated at the sound of someone moving around in the bedroom.

"It's Roy," Karyn said. "Do you think we should tell him?"

Inez shrugged noncommittally as Roy came into the

room pulling a sweater on over his head. "Hello, Inez," he said. Then, to Karyn, "Is there any coffee?"

"I can make a new pot."

"Never mind. Fresh air is what I really need."

"Roy, can we talk to you about something?"

"Will it keep? I'm still groggy from last night. If I jog down the road and back it might wake me up."

Karyn hesitated a moment. "Go ahead. It's not important."

"I'll see you later." He went out the door, and they heard him trot off across the clearing and down the road.

"I just couldn't tell him," Karyn said. "Not yet."

"All right," said Inez.

Karyn clapped her hands together and stood up. "I guess it's you and me, pal. Let's head for town and find the guy with only one ear."

CHAPTER
SIXTEEN

~~~~~~

The two women left the house and walked across the grass to Inez' little Plymouth Valiant. They got in and Inez fastened her seat belt.

"You'll have to buckle up too," she told Karyn. "This is a '74, the model that doesn't start unless everybody is properly strapped in."

"I feel silly," Karyn said as they drove to Drago. "This whole idea is beginning to seem silly."

"It can't hurt to look. We might get lucky. We could ask around too, if there's somebody you know well enough to talk to."

"The only one I can think of is Oriole Jolivet. She and her husband run the general store."

"Can we trust her?"

"I wouldn't want to come right out and tell her we're looking for a werewolf," Karyn said. "But then I wouldn't want to admit that to anybody."

The store was empty when Karyn and Inez walked in. After a minute Karyn walked to the back and called Oriole's name.

"Be with you in a minute," came Oriole's answer from the back room.

Inez strolled around the cluttered store looking at the merchandise while they waited. In a little while Oriole Jolivet came out and joined them. She wore a cotton dress with a big flower print that made her look even wider than she was. Her hair was pinned back, and Karyn was secretly relieved to see no sign of a head wound.

"Hey, how's Roy doing?" Oriole asked after the introductions had been completed. "I'll tell you, Karyn, if I was twenty years younger I'd give you a little competition for that handsome sonofagun." She laughed heartily to show she was only kidding.

"That's really why I'm here, Oriole," Karyn said, improvising quickly. "Roy cut his hand yesterday chopping firewood, and I need some bandages if you carry them." She was surprised how easily the lie came to her lips.

Oriole's smile switched instantly to a concerned frown. "Gee, I'm sorry to hear that. I hope it's not too serious."

"I don't think so," Karyn said, a little ashamed now of her deceit. "It's a clean cut. No infection. I did want to get some bandages to wrap it, though."

"Sure, we got bandages," Oriole said, moving to the far side of the store. She stooped to one of the lower shelves. "What-all do you need—cotton, gauze, adhesive?"

"You'd better give me the works."

Oriole removed the selected items from the shelf and put them in a paper bag. "A person has to be darned careful using an ax."

"I guess it's lucky you have this stuff." Karyn kept her tone as casual as she could. "I don't suppose there's any-place else in town I could get it."

"Nope. Not in Drago."

"You must sell quite a few medical supplies."

"Not so much. People around here are pretty healthy."

Karyn did not know how to go any further without blurting out an obvious question. Oriole saved her the trouble by volunteering the information. "The last time I sold any bandages was last spring when the Eccles boy stuck his arm through a window without opening it first." She tapped her forehead. "The boy's fifteen years old now, but up here he's still about three."

Karyn and Inez laughed uneasily and looked at each other. Their best source for town gossip had come up dry.

Karyn paid for the purchases and started out of the store. Passing the glassed meat case she suddenly realized she had not seen Oriole's silent husband today.

"Where's Etienne?" she said, turning back to Oriole.

"He didn't come in today. Woke up this morning with a headache."

"A headache?" Karyn repeated, carefully keeping the excitement out of her voice.

"It's no big deal. He gets 'em two, three times a year. They last a day or two, then go away."

"I hope he gets better soon."

"He will."

"Tell him hello for me."

"I'll do that. Come again when you can stay awhile. You too, Inez."

"What do you think?" Karyn said, when they were outside and out of earshot.

"It's a possibility. At least we have a suspect now. Before we had nothing." Inez grew thoughtful. "I have a feeling the two of us shouldn't try to take this any further without help. Is there no one else in town we could go to?"

"No . . . Wait a minute. We forgot the most logical person—the town doctor."

"The one who treated you?"

"Yes. Dr. Volkmann. If someone was seriously injured he wouldn't go to the store for treatment."

"Makes sense. Can we talk to him frankly?"

"As you said, we've got to talk to somebody some-time."

"Then let's go and see him. If we get good vibrations we'll tell him the story. If not, well, we'll try something else."

Dr. Volkmann received the women graciously and showed them into the sitting room of his big old house. The influence of his late wife could still be seen in touches like the lace antimacassars on the backs of chairs, and the little animal figurines carefully arranged, but undusted now, on corner shelves.

"You're looking well, Mrs. Beatty," the doctor said. "Did you use all of the pills I gave you?"

"No, I don't think I need any more of them."

"That's good. Too much reliance on pills can be dan-gerous." He folded his hands and waited politely.

"What we came for is . . . well, I'd like to ask you a question, Doctor."

"Certainly."

"Did anyone come to you last night or today for treat-ment of a head wound?"

"Etienne Jolivet in particular," Inez added.

Volkmann studied the women for several seconds be-fore he spoke. "That's an odd question. Do you mind telling me what's behind it?"

"Believe me," Karyn said, "it's very important."

"I can see that it is. The answer is no, I have not treated anyone for head wounds in the past forty-eight hours. I have not treated Etienne Jolivet for anything in more than three years."

Karyn's face reflected her disappointment.

"Now do you suppose I could have an explanation?"

The women's eyes met, and they made a decision.

"I'll tell you, Doctor," Karyn said, "but you might not believe it."

"Let's hear it, anyway," said Volkmann. His voice was deep and serious and reassuring.

Karyn told him the whole story, beginning with the first time she had heard the howling, and ending with the visit a few minutes before to the Jolivets' store. When Karyn was through, Inez told him about the clippings she had saved detailing strange happenings in and around Drago over the years.

Dr. Volkmann listened intently, and did not interrupt. When the women had finished their story he sat silently, studying them.

"So when you heard of Etienne Jolivet's headache," he said finally, "you felt it might be the result of the gunshot wound inflicted on the wolf last night."

Karyn nodded, not meeting Volkmann's eye. It all seemed so farfetched when put into words by someone else.

"I am afraid you settled your suspicions on the wrong man. Etienne has suffered all his life from migraine headaches, just as Oriole told you."

"And there was nobody else with a head injury of any kind?"

"No one came to me, at any rate."

Karyn's shoulders slumped. "What do you think, Doctor? Am I crazy? Are we a couple of hysterical women? Was it all a dream?"

Again Volkmann took his time in answering. "I have lived here in Drago for ten years. I have lived quietly, and have had ample opportunity to observe the town and its people. During those ten years I have noted a number of strange occurrences. Some of them, Miss Polk, were those that you mentioned. People have died and disappeared in this valley with no reasonable explanation ever given. I must confess that I closed my eyes to a number of . . . irregularities that I might have questioned had I been a more involved man. But I was wrapped up in my own affairs. It is, of course, possible that there is something fearfully wrong here."

Inez spoke up. "And what do you think, Doctor, of the idea that it is a werewolf?"

Volkmann's expression remained grave. "As a man of science I am not willing to admit to the existence of something so far outside the laws of nature. However, as a man who has seen more than the normal share of inexplicable happenings, I cannot deny the possibility. Yes, Miss Polk, there may be a werewolf."

"Thank God you believe us," Karyn said.

Volkmann held up a cautioning hand. "This does not mean I am ready to join you in an all-out hunt for the alleged werewolf. I still have serious reservations. I will do what I can, though, to assist you in gathering information. You may call on me at any time."

"Thank you, Doctor," said Inez. "I can't tell you how much it means to have someone else on our side."

Dr. Volkmann walked them to the door. "Have you spoken to anyone else about this?" he asked.

"No," Karyn said. "Only you."

"I think it would be wise to keep it that way. At least until we have something more to go on."

"That's the way we felt too," Karyn said.

"Let me know if anything else happens. And one other thing, ladies . . ."

"Yes?"

"Be careful."

Karyn and Inez assured the doctor they would be most careful, and walked back to where they had left the car.

They got in, went through the ritual of buckling the seat belts and started home. As Inez reached Karyn's road, Karyn put a hand on her arm.

"Wait a minute. Can you drive back up the street the way we came?"

"Why?"

"I want you to take a look at the man standing back there under the theater marquee."

"The one with the hat?"

"Yes."

Inez backed around and drove slowly up the street. "Who is it?" she said as they approached the figure standing in the shadow of the marquee.

"Anton Gadak," Karyn said.

As they rolled past they could see a fresh white bandage covering the left side of Gadak's head.

Inez started to wheel the car around.

"Where are you going?" Karyn said.

"Back to the doctor's house. We should tell him about this."

"Let's wait," Karyn said.

"But why?"

"Who do you suppose applied that bandage?"

CHAPTER
SEVENTEEN

Inez braked the car to a stop in front of Karyn's house. She left the engine idling, and the women sat for a minute without speaking.

"I'm going to tell Roy," Karyn said. "I've got to."

"Yes, I suppose you do."

"It isn't going to be easy. He's always so level-headed and practical. I've got to try, though."

"I understand," Inez said.

Karyn smiled and gave the other woman's hand a squeeze. She left Inez waiting in the car and ran across the clearing to the house. She found Roy inside at the table. He was bent over a manuscript, making corrections with a red pencil.

"Roy, can I talk to you?"

"Is it important? I really want to finish these books tonight."

"It's important."

With a sigh Roy laid the pencil aside and shifted the chair around so he was facing her. "All right."

Karyn hesitated. Now that she had Roy's full attention, she felt foolish. She did not know where to start, how to convince him that she was deadly serious. She decided that to plunge right in was as good a way as any.

"Roy, do you know what a werewolf is?"

"Did you say werewolf?"

"Yes."

"A guy who turns into a wolf when the moon is full and runs around growling and eating people. Right?"

"Close."

"So what's the point?"

Karyn drew a deep breath. "I believe there is a werewolf in Drago."

"Oh, uh-huh. And this was important enough to interrupt my work?"

"I'm serious, damn you."

"All right, Karyn, let's hear the rest of it."

"I believe there is a werewolf in Drago. I believe the werewolf killed our dog, killed the two kids who came hiking through here the other day, and killed God knows how many others."

Roy was watching her, his face carefully expressionless.

"I believe the werewolf is Anton Gadak."

"Ah, Jesus, Karyn . . ."

"Listen to me. Last night I shot that huge wolf out in front of the house. You saw the blood, you found a piece of its ear. Today I saw Anton Gadak in town. He has a fresh bandage covering the left side of his head."

Roy stared incredulously. "And on the basis of that you have decided that Anton Gadak is a . . . a werewolf?"

"It's not only that, Roy. Through the years there have been lots of strange disappearances and unexplained deaths around Drago. Who would be in a better position to cover up what really happened than Gadak?"

"'Wait a minute. What's all this about strange deaths and disappearances? You make this sound like the Bermuda Triangle."

"It's true. Inez Polk has clippings from local newspapers."

"I might have known."

"Roy, don't you hear what I'm telling you? Anton Gadak is a werewolf."

Roy jumped out of the chair and spread his arms. "What the hell do you want me to do? Go into town and drive a stake through his heart?"

"I want you to believe me, that's all."

"Those pills you've been taking . . ."

"I haven't had a pill in two days."

Roy searched her eyes, as though looking for signs of madness. Finally he said, "All right, Karyn, I'll tell you what we're going to do. We're going to get the hell out of here and go back to Los Angeles. That ought to satisfy you."

"Roy, I didn't mean—"

"You can start packing now. We'll leave tomorrow and move into a motel or something in L.A. until I can make other arrangements." He started out the door.

"Where are you going?"

"Into town to settle our bills. I want to get away as soon as possible."

Karyn stood in the center of the room feeling stunned as Roy slammed out of the house. She had handled it badly, but there was no justification for Roy's sudden anger. She had not expected him to instantly accept the idea, but she had counted on being able to discuss it with him. The thought of running back to Los Angeles now seemed wrong. It left an unpaid debt to Neal Edwards and Pam Sealander. And to nameless others who would follow.

Feeling numb and defeated, Karyn left the house and walked slowly across the small clearing to where Inez waited standing beside the car.

"I guess it didn't go too well," said Inez.

"It went badly," Karyn said.

"He didn't believe you?"

"He wouldn't even listen to me. He thinks I'm hallucinating. Could he be right, Inez? Is it possible there is something wrong with my mind?"

"There's nothing wrong with you, Karyn. If you're crazy, so am I."

"Roy might agree with that too."

"Very possibly. He didn't even look at me when he stormed out of the house. Where was he going, anyway?"

"Into town to pay our bills. We're going back to Los Angeles tomorrow."

"Oh?"

"I feel that I'm running out on you."

"Don't be silly. It might be the best thing for you."

For a moment the two women faced each other, then Inez put her arms around Karyn. They clung together like sisters.

"Take care of yourself," Inez said.

"You too."

A little self-consciously they moved apart. Inez put her hand on the car door handle.

"Well . . . goodbye," said Inez.

"Goodbye. We'll be in touch, won't we?"

"Of course."

Even as they spoke, Karyn could see in the other woman's eyes that neither of them believed it. After Drago they would never again see each other.

Inez got into her car and drove off down the road without looking back. Karyn went into the house and sat down to wait for Roy. Suddenly she was very tired.

CHAPTER EIGHTEEN

When he was a hundred yards down the grassy road toward the village, Roy Beatty slowed down. His anger had melted away, and he was ashamed of the way he had spoken to Karyn. He reminded himself what she had been through, and that the only reason they came to this isolated valley was to help her. The last thing in the world he should be doing now was losing his temper and storming out of the house like some sulky adolescent.

But a *werewolf!* It had to be, Roy decided, Inez Polk who was putting such ideas into Karyn's head. He wished now that he had gone over to the car when he came out of the house and had it out with the woman. But at the time he had been too angry. All he wanted to do was get away.

Well, no, that was not quite right. His real reason for going to the village, he had to admit, was to see Marcia

Lura one more time. He would have to tell Marcia he was leaving. It would not be easy, but it was impossible to simply go without seeing her again. His emotional bond to the green-eyed woman was too strong to allow that. Roy could not put a name to the emotion between him and Marcia. Not love, certainly, not in the sense that he loved Karyn. Lust was more accurate. Sheer physical attraction. Chemistry. And yet there was more to it than that. Marcia Lura had introduced him to sensual delights that were beyond anything he had experienced. Beyond anything he had imagined. No, it would not be easy to leave what he had found here.

Roy came to the main road that led into the village. As he turned and walked toward the gift shop he tried and rejected a number of opening remarks for what he must say to Marcia. There was no way to soften it.

In a way, he told himself, it was good that this business with Karyn had come up now. Eventually he would have had to break off with Marcia, and the longer he put it off, the more difficult it would be. Her hold on him would grow with every meeting. It was like a strange sweet sickness.

The village of Drago was bright and empty. Eddies of dust curled along the main street in the light breeze. The shadows of afternoon had barely begun to darken the valley. Roy turned at Marcia Lura's gift shop and pushed in through the door.

The bell over the door tinkled, an incongruously merry sound that did not match his mood. He peered around in the perpetually dim light of the shop.

Marcia came in through the curtains in the rear that separated the shop from her living quarters. She wore tight-fitting pants that hugged her thighs and belled out at the ankles. A striped blouse was open several buttons down, revealing an amulet on a gold chain that hung in the crevice between her breasts.

"Hello, Roy," she said. "I wasn't expecting you until later."

For a moment he stood looking at her without speaking. Her pale-green eyes were softly luminous in the dusk. The black hair had an animal sheen to it that reflected blue highlights. She was so beautiful it brought a lump to his throat.

"I have to talk to you, Marcia," he said finally.

"All right. Come in the back." She reached out a slim arm to part the curtains.

For a moment Roy hesitated. Somewhere deep in his subconsciousness a warning sounded, but the nearness of the woman, the heat of her body, the scent of her, overpowered his doubts. He walked through the curtain into her rooms.

"I was having some tea," she said. "Let me make you a cup."

Without waiting for him to answer, Marcia went to her small gas range and turned up the flame under a copper teakettle. From a canister she spooned crumbled leaves into a cup, then added a few drops of thick liquid from an opaque bottle. Roy watched, fascinated by the grace of even her smallest movements.

When the water was boiling Marcia poured it into the cup and stirred the mixture. She carried the cup across the room and set it on a low table before the sofa.

"Let the tea steep for a minute before you drink it," she said. She sat down on the sofa, patting the cushion next to her.

Roy sat down beside her, but was careful not to let their bodies touch. To keep from looking into her eyes, he busied himself stirring the tea. Its aroma was a mixture of spices with a hint of something bitter.

"You wanted to talk to me," Marcia said.

"Yes."

"About us?"

"In a way. And about Karyn. She isn't getting any better."

"I'm sorry."

"So am I. I'm going to have to take her away from here."

"You're leaving Drago?"

"I have to."

For the briefest fraction of a second Marcia's body stiffened. The pale-green eyes narrowed, and Roy saw a flash there of something dark and dangerous. Then it was gone. Marcia was poised again, cool and lovely, and Roy thought he must have imagined the moment.

"How soon must you go?" Her throaty voice was without emotion.

"Tomorrow."

"I see. Your tea should be ready to drink now."

Roy looked down at the cup as though wondering where it had come from. He lifted it to his lips and sipped the dark brew. It had a sweet, wild taste.

"Do you like it?" she asked. "It's a very old recipe."

"It's fine," he said quickly. "Marcia, I don't want to talk about the tea."

"About what, then?"

"I hate to leave you. Do you know that?"

"I know," she said. "But we never pretended it was forever, did we?"

"No, but I want you to know that it wasn't just a . . . a fling for me. You've been something very special in my life. You've given me something I've never known. I'll never forget you, Marcia."

Marcia leaned toward him. Again he had the delicious sensation of being drawn into those deep green eyes. Into them and down to unknown depths.

"No," she said softly. "You never will forget me. Drink your tea, darling."

He raised the cup and drank. The pungent steam brought tears to his eyes. When he put the cup back down in the saucer he was surprised to see that his hand was shaking.

Marcia watched him. She reached over and placed her hand on his leg. The fingers seemed to sear his flesh through the cloth. His world shrank to this room and this hour and this woman.

He touched her hair. His hand moved to the back of her neck and pulled her head toward him. They kissed, their mouths open, tongues mating. When at last he pulled back a little way, Roy was breathing heavily.

"I do love you, Marcia," he said.

She shook her head. "No. You admire me. You want me. You may even need me. But you do not love me."

Roy started to say something more, but she stopped him.

"Not yet," she said. "You do not love me yet. But you will, my Roy, you will."

He kissed her again. His hand moved down the long smooth curve of her back to her firm, round hip. Marcia's body moved under his hand, and he felt that she was wearing nothing beneath the blouse and pants.

Marcia drew back her head and looked into his eyes. The corners of her mouth curled upward in the suggestion of a smile.

"Tell me what you want, Roy." She ran her tongue across her teeth. "Tell me what you want to do to me."

"I want to make love to you," he said.

"Not like that. Tell me in the real words. The words you say to me when we are naked together."

"I want to fuck you."

"Yes. Yes. And what else?"

"I want to taste you."

"Where?"

"Your breasts. Your nipples. Your cunt. I want to kiss you and taste you there and everywhere."

"And do you want to be inside me?"

"Yes. Oh, yes."

"Tell me."

"I want to be inside you. Deep inside. All the way."

"And do you want me to take it in my mouth?"

"Yes."

"And roll my tongue around it and kiss it and suck the sweet drops from it?"

"Oh, God, Marcia, yes!"

All rational thought was driven from Roy's mind by his pounding desire. With every fiber of his being he wanted to possess this black-haired, smooth-limbed woman. He wanted her sexually, carnally, totally. Nothing else was real. At that moment, had it been necessary, Roy Beatty would have killed to get her.

Marcia slipped out of his grasp and stood up. She undid the remaining buttons of her blouse, stripped it from her shoulders, and tossed it away, paying no attention to where it fell. She moved back in front of Roy and leaned down to put a hand on each of his knees. As he sat looking up at her, she spread his legs and stepped between them. She moved her hands then to the back of his neck. Clasping her fingers there, she pulled his face forward into the soft, warm valley of her breasts.

Roy inhaled the mingled musk and sandalwood. He tasted the salt of her flesh and the metal of the amulet she wore. He bit down on the soft chain and it snapped. The amulet fell softly to the carpet.

Marcia backed away from him again, and Roy stood up, fumbling with his clothes. His erection thrust forward like a lance.

Quickly Marcia unzipped the pants she wore and slipped them down her long legs and off. She stood before him smoothly naked, proud of her body. Roy moved toward her, but she stopped him with a gentle hand on his chest. Watching his face, she let her free hand dip down between them. The fingers curled around his penis.

"You are ready for me, my man," she said. "Aren't you?"

"I'm ready," he whispered.

She released him, turned her back, and dropped suddenly to her hands and knees. "Then ride me, my lover. Ride me!"

With the blood roaring in his head, Roy went to his knees behind her. She raised her buttocks to him. He thrust forward and penetrated. At once he started to withdraw.

"No," she commanded. "Leave it there. Give it to me there."

With his hands planted on Marcia's ivory-smooth cheeks, Roy drove into her a centimeter at a time. She let her head sink to the floor, the side of her face pressed against the carpet. To meet each of his thrusts she pushed back with her hips. From deep in her throat came a soft growling moan.

With a final painful shove Roy buried the full length of his organ in her. There he was held fast, as though gripped by burning fingers. He knew that at any second he would climax up there.

"No," she said. The single syllable held him like a physical barrier.

They froze in position. The excruciating sensuality made him want to cry out, but he knew any movement would bring on the explosion. Marcia raised her head and turned to look at him. Her eyes blazed green.

"We aren't through with each other yet, are we, my lover?"

Fraction by slow tight fraction he withdrew. Half a dozen times he was an eyeblink from climax, but each time Marcia's phenomenal control of her muscles stopped him, held him in check, until at last he was out of her.

During the timeless span that followed, Marcia Lura led Roy along paths of physical joy he had never traveled. With unfailing instinct she did exactly the right thing at exactly the right moment. By turns she submitted to him wholly, then took the lead and became the aggressor.

Sexual fantasies locked in Roy's mind since childhood sprang to vivid life. Time and again he would be at the brink of orgasm, and each time Marcia would stop him just short of total release and bring him back.

The shadows of evening moved into the valley and darkened the windows of Marcia's small apartment, but the people within had no sense of time. For Roy Beatty the universe consisted of the hills and hollows, the knowing hands, and the wet, clinging orifices of the wild black-haired woman.

When at last she brought him to the finish he was in a kneeling position. She lay on her back with her head away from him, her elbows propped on the floor, her legs scissored behind his back. Their movement, in and out, together and apart, was not more than an inch. Marcia's eyes never left his face.

"Now!" she said suddenly. And again, "Nowwwwww!" drawing it out in a husky growl.

Roy let go, and the explosion pulled him inside out. It was like being born, and it was like dying. Every good sensation of his life was jammed into the heaving, sweating climax. He spurted hot and hard and emptied himself into her. They cried out together, and their cry became a scream, and at last it was finished.

Roy fell back, and for long, long minutes he lay motionless on the soft carpet. It was as though all the nerves of his body had been severed. He had not enough strength to make a fist.

Marcia slid up to lie beside him. He did not open his eyes, but he could smell her, smell the sex of her and their mingled sweat, and still the gentle sandalwood. He wanted to cry. Then he felt the tears slide down his face and he knew he was crying.

"Marcia . . ."

"Hush." She stopped his lips with her fingers.

"But I want to tell you—"

"No, there is nothing more to be said. It is time now

for you to go." She moved away from him.

Slowly Roy sat up. He felt drained. Empty. Across the room Marcia lit a candle, and for the first time he realized night had come.

She walked around gathering up his clothes and brought them to him. He dressed silently and methodically while she sat in the shadows watching him. When he was finished dressing he crossed to the back door. There he hesitated and turned, wanting to say something to her. She shook her head no, and he went out and closed the door behind him.

Walking home along the path through the woods, Roy fought against the still-fresh memory of what had happened to him this night. He knew he must not think about it now. Maybe not ever. Not if he was to live a normal life again.

To keep his mind busy he tried concentrating on the problems of his work. No good. His work was too far away, and the feel of Marcia's body was still on his skin. But he must not think of her. He recited the Greek alphabet aloud. Forward first, then backward.

"Omega, psi, chi, phi, upsilon . . ." He stopped. He was being followed.

The sound was a soft, rhythmic thud as of something trotting after him on padded paws. Roy peered back along the path where moonlight filtered down through the trees to make bright patches on the trail. As he watched, a lean shadow moved swiftly through one of the pools of moonlight.

As the shadow loped through the next patch of light Roy saw what it was. A wolf. But more than a wolf. A long-bodied black creature moving toward him with power and assurance. Its mouth was drawn back in a grotesque animal grin. And the eyes. The eyes knew him.

Before Roy could react the beast pushed off with powerful hind legs and hit him full in the chest. He staggered back under the blow and instinctively wrapped his arms around the animal. The strength of the beast was unnatural. He could feel the play of its muscles under the thick fur. The wolf's hind feet dug into the dirt and it forced Roy steadily backward.

The face of the wolf was only an inch from his own. Its breath, hot and damp, hissed in his ear. The glistening teeth, as long as two of his finger joints, snapped at the air and moved closer to his throat.

Inexorably, a step at a time, Roy was forced back by the superior strength of the wolf. He clutched at the thick neck fur, but could not pull the thing's face away from his. As he was pushed back off the path, Roy's foot caught in a tangle of fern and he crashed to the ground on his back.

With the beast astride him now, Roy flailed at it with his fists, but his blows had no more effect than those of a baby. The thin black lips of the wolf stretched in a snarl of triumph.

While Roy still struggled to free himself, the wolf's head dipped and the cruel teeth bit effortlessly through his shirt and the flesh of his shoulder. Through the explosion of pain Roy could hear the teeth grating on bone. His right arm went dead, and his will to resist died with it.

In his last moment of consciousness Roy looked into the face of the wolf. The muzzle was smeared now with bright fresh blood. And again the eyes. He knew the eyes. And he knew he was lost. Roy arched his neck, baring his throat to the killer teeth.

CHAPTER NINETEEN

~~~~~~

Roy lay with his eyes closed, waiting for the final burst of agony that would come when the teeth of the wolf ripped away his throat. Incredibly, nothing happened. He forced his eyes open and saw the beast, bloody-mouthed, watching him. The cruel mouth stretched again in a triumphant snarl. Then the beast backed off, turned to the forest, and slipped away into the night.

Minutes went by and there was only the darkness and the sounds of the small forest creatures. Roy tried to rise, but the pain in his shoulder was like a hot iron. His mind would not work. Thoughts crumbled into fragments of visions, making no sense, forming no pattern. With his body operating on instinct alone, he began to crawl through the brush. He crawled until finally he was back on the path. With a wrenching effort he raised himself to his feet. With his right arm dangling he stumbled along the path toward his house. Again and again he fell heavily to the ground, but each time he rose again to stagger on.

Something jolted Karyn Beatty out of her sleep. She looked around, disoriented for a moment. She was in the living room of the little house. In the rocking chair by the window. She must have dozed off. What was she doing out here? Waiting for Roy, that was it. She remembered then, sitting here through the afternoon, waiting while he did not return. She had opened a can of soup for her dinner, then sat down again. Then she must have fallen asleep.

The gray luminescence of the window through the curtain told her it was dawn. She had slept here through the night, and Roy was still not home.

What had awakened her? A noise outside the house. Something out there. She hurried to the closet where the shotgun was kept and brought it back into the living room. Cautiously she unlocked the front door and opened it just enough to look out. The sky was lightening, but the forest was still dark and secret beyond the clearing. There seemed to be nothing . . . then she looked down. There at her feet, his body twisted into an awkward position, lay her husband.

Quickly Karyn put the gun down inside the house and knelt beside Roy. His clothes and his hair were covered with pine needles, twigs, and dirt. He was alive, but flushed and feverish. His breathing was shallow, his face damp with perspiration.

"Roy, my God, what's happened to you?"

There was no reply.

Karyn cradled Roy's head in her lap. His eyes fluttered open. For an instant they had a look of unspeakable terror and she felt his entire body go rigid. Then his expression clouded and he relaxed. His eyes were still open, but he seemed to see nothing.

"Roy, what is it? What happened to you? Oh, please answer me!"

His eyes closed again, then opened with the same blank expression. With her hands under his arms Karyn managed to heave him to his feet and steer him into the house. She got him into the bedroom and eased him into a sitting position on the bed. When she pushed him gently back he lay down without resistance. She took off his shoes and loosened his belt. His shirt was badly torn at the shoulder and stained with what looked like blood, but there was no wound underneath.

Karyn covered him with a blanket, pulling it high around his shoulders.

"Roy . . . Roy, I'm going for the doctor. Can you hear me?"

He groaned deep in his chest—a sound that might or might not have been an answer.

"You stay here and keep warm. I'll be back as soon as I can."

Karyn ran out of the house. The sun was visible now through a gap in the mountains, slanting down through the trees, warming the shadowed places.

For one of the few times in her life Karyn truly regretted that she had never learned to drive. There in the clearing sat the Ford—so accessible, so ready, so useless to her. She considered for a moment taking it anyway and trying somehow to drive it as far as Drago. She had sat next to Roy often enough to know the procedures. But no, it would be foolish now to risk smashing up the car on top of the other urgent problems. She began to run down the narrow lane toward the village.

She ran until she was out of breath, then walked, then ran again. Soon she reached the blacktopped road and turned toward Drago. No one was out in the early morning. She had the town to herself.

The street where Dr. Volkmann lived was still in shadow. The window blinds in the house were drawn. The doctor's dusty old Buick stood in the driveway. Karyn ran up the wooden steps to the porch and rang the bell. She waited a minute, then rang again. This time she heard someone moving inside.

Dr. Volkmann opened the door and blinked down at her. He wore a faded blue bathrobe and slippers with no backs. His thin gray hair was in disarray.

"Why, Karyn, what is it?"

"Something's happened to Roy, Doctor. Can you come and see him?"

"Happened? What's happened?"

"I don't know. He went into town yesterday afternoon. I fell asleep in a chair waiting for him. A little while ago a noise woke me up and I went to the door. Roy was just outside lying on the ground."

As she finished speaking Karyn began to sob, the pent-up emotion breaking through.

"I'll be right with you," said the doctor. He reached into his worn bag on the hall table and took out a bottle. He shook two pills into his hand and gave them to Karyn. "In the meantime you'd better take these. They'll calm your nerves. You can take them with a glass of water from the kitchen while I'm getting dressed."

Karyn walked down the musty hallway to a large, old-fashioned kitchen. She found a drinking glass in one of the cupboards and ran it full of water. She looked down at the pills and hesitated. No more of these, she reminded herself. She dropped the pills down the sink drain and poured the water after them. She walked back into the front hall in time to meet the doctor coming down the stairs. He wore a sweater and pants and shoes hastily pulled on over his bare feet.

"Let's go," he said.

Volkmann snatched up the medical bag and he and Karyn hurried out to the old Buick. It started at once, and Volkmann gunned the engine up the street to the road that turned off toward the Beattys' house.

"What were Roy's symptoms when you found him?" the doctor asked.

"He was only semi-conscious. His face was all red and he felt as though he had a fever. He opened his eyes, but they didn't seem to focus on anything."

"And when you left?"

"I put him in the bed. He seemed to be sleeping, but his breathing was uneven and his body seemed tense."

"Any marks or injuries?"

"That's a curious thing. His shirt looked as though it was stained with blood, but there was no wound that could have bled like that. Only scratches on his hands and face that could have come from the brush. There might be something else. I didn't undress him."

Volkmann pulled the Buick in behind Roy's Ford, and he and Karyn went into the house. Roy was still in the bed where Karyn had left him. His eyes were closed. His head rolled fitfully on the pillow.

"Help me get his clothes off," said Volkmann, "and we'll give him a going-over for injuries."

Roy made feeble sounds of protest as Karyn and Dr. Volkmann pulled off his clothes, but he did not wake up. The doctor examined him thoroughly from head to foot, then rolled him onto his stomach and checked his back. He probed delicately through the blond hair on Roy's head, and finally looked up at Karyn.

"No apparent injuries anywhere. His symptoms are similar to those of a concussion, and that might be the case even though there is no sign of a blow on the head."

Together they rolled Roy over on his back again, and Karyn covered him with the blanket. As she did so, he opened his eyes and looked at her.

"Karyn," he said thickly. "What time is it?" Then his expression became more alert. He raised his head. "Dr. Volkmann, why are you here? What happened?"

"We were hoping you could tell us," said the doctor.

Karyn took Roy's hand and pressed it against her cheek. "Darling, are you all right?"

"I—I think so. I feel a little shaky. Confused. What's going on?"

"You went into Drago yesterday afternoon and didn't return," Volkmann said. "This morning your wife found you lying outside the door. She came to get me."

Roy frowned with the effort of trying to remember. "Let's see . . . I was working here in the afternoon—was that yesterday?—when Karyn came home. We talked about . . . Damn, I can't remember what we talked about. An argument, I think. I don't know." He rubbed his eyes with his fingertips before going on. "That's it. After that I fade out. The next thing I remember is looking up and seeing the two of you standing over me just now."

"You don't remember anything about last night?" Karyn prompted.

Roy shook his head. "There was sort of a dream." His eyes looked far away for a moment, then he went on. "I remember something about an animal. And eyes. Eyes that I knew, yet didn't know. Doesn't make much sense, does it?" He turned to Volkmann. "What's the matter with me, Doctor?"

"As far as I can determine you have no serious injuries. Still, I'd like you to come into town for an examination when you're feeling up to it."

"If you think it's necessary. Actually I feel pretty good now. Just awfully tired and a little fuzzy in the head."

"I think you should sleep now. Perhaps when you awaken your memory will return."

"I hope so," Roy said. His speech was beginning to slur as his eyes lost their focus.

Karyn stayed behind for a moment as the doctor went out to the living room. She drew the curtain across the window, then came back and sat down carefully on the edge of the bed.

"I'll be right in the next room if you need me," she said.

Without warning Roy's eyes snapped wide open. Karyn recoiled as for an instant she looked into the haunted face of a stranger. Then his features went slack and his eyes closed in uneasy sleep. It had happened so fast Karyn could not be sure she hadn't imagined it. She backed away from the bed and went out. Softly she closed the door behind her.

Dr. Volkmann, waiting in the living room, was quick to reassure her. "Your husband will be all right," he said. "What he needs is rest and quiet."

"We were talking about going back to Los Angeles," Karyn said, "but he doesn't seem to remember."

"It's up to you, of course, but I don't think the added pressure of going back to the city right now would help his condition."

"I suppose we'll stay now, at least until he's better. Doctor . . ." Karyn hesitated, searching for the words. "Do you think it's possible Roy could have been attacked by . . . by . . ."

"By the werewolf?"

Karyn nodded.

"You saw his body. There were no wounds."

"Could it have come after him and he escaped?"

"We have no way of knowing what happened. In the morning you might question him some more about that dream he mentioned. But be gentle. He's not in any condition to be quizzed about a werewolf."

"Doctor, I have to ask you something."

"Yes?"

"Have you treated Anton Gadak in the last couple of days?"

"No. Why?"

"Do you remember I told you about wounding the wolf out in front of the house?"

"I remember. You thought at the time it might have been Etienne Jolivet."

"Yes, until you explained about his migraines."

"What has this to do with Anton Gadak?"

"As Inez Polk and I drove away from your house we saw Gadak on the street. He had a bandage covering one side of his head. And the ear."

"Why didn't you come to me at once?"

"To tell the truth, we thought you might be involved."

"Because you thought I'd put the bandage on and not told you about it, is that it?"

"Yes."

"Well, I didn't, but I can understand your caution. Nevertheless, we'd be better off to trust each other. I'll find out what I can about Anton Gadak's injury. Meanwhile, you be very careful."

"You don't have to worry about that."

"You should be in no danger in the daytime, but if you can avoid it, don't go out after dark alone."

Karyn saw Dr. Volkmann to the door and watched him start back toward Drago. Then she returned to the bedroom and looked at Roy. He was sleeping peacefully enough, except for a nerve that twitched at the corner of one eye.

Throughout the day Karyn kept watch while Roy continued to sleep. By nightfall she was exhausted. She undressed and slipped into bed next to him, being careful not to disturb him. She was so tired she dropped off in minutes.

Sometime during the night she was pulled up out of a dreamless sleep. Roy sat stiffly upright beside her, his eyes wide open, staring at emptiness.

"Roy, what is it?"

Then she heard, in the woods not far away, the howling.

CHAPTER TWENTY

~~~~~~

Karyn did not sleep again until it was almost dawn. When next she awoke, Roy lay quietly beside her. His eyes were closed, but the frown line between his brows showed he was awake.

"Good morning, darling," she said softly.

He rolled his head on the pillow and looked at her. "Hello, Karyn."

"How are you feeling?"

"So-so."

"Are you hungry? Would you like me to bring you some breakfast?"

Roy sat up suddenly and pushed the covers away. "No. Stop treating me like an invalid. I've got to get up and do some work."

"Dr. Volkmann said you should rest."

"Doctors always say that. You rest. I've got work to do."

Karyn got out of bed on her own side. "If that's what you want. But try not to tire yourself."

She prepared a big breakfast of buttermilk pancakes with fried eggs and thick country bacon. Roy only toyed with his food. He answered Karyn's attempts at conversation with monosyllables. His thoughts were far away.

"You should eat something," Karyn said. "You didn't have any dinner last night. Did you?"

"I'm just not very hungry," he said, attempting a smile. "It wouldn't hurt me to take off a few pounds anyway."

Karyn looked across the table into the shadowed eyes of her husband and said nothing. This was a mood she had never seen.

Roy got up, leaving most of the food on his plate, and waited impatiently while Karyn cleared the dishes from the table. Then he spread out his papers and sat down to work. Karyn kept out of the way, but watched him. He grew increasingly restless, cursing at the manuscripts in front of him, scribbling angrily on the pages. Before an hour had passed he threw down the pencil and expelled his breath in exasperation.

"Dammit, there are pages missing. You'd think that somebody would check this garbage before they send it to me. I can't edit what's not here."

"Why don't you take a break?" Karyn suggested.

Roy slammed both hands flat on the table and stood up. He paced back and forth across the room with his fists jammed into his pockets.

"Wouldn't you like to lie down for a while?" Karyn said.

"No, I wouldn't like to lie down for a while," he answered, mimicking her voice. "I'm going out."

Without waiting for a response from Karyn he threw open the door and stalked out of the house. She watched him cross the clearing and take one of the forest paths.

When Roy was out of sight she walked back to the table and leafed through the pages of the manuscript. They were all there.

She dropped into a chair and stared down at her hands. Things seemed to be closing in, pressing her down, stifling her breath.

The morning dragged into afternoon. Roy came home in the same irritable mood as when he had left. He refused lunch and sat down to try to work again. It was painful for Karyn to watch.

"Roy, do you think we ought to go in and see Dr. Volkmann?"

"What for?"

"He said he'd like to see you again if you were feeling well enough."

"What's the matter, didn't you pay him for yesterday?"

"That's not fair. He's been very good about coming out when we need him."

"Well, we don't need him now." Roy drew a long, heavy sigh, then got up and came over to Karyn. "You're right, I shouldn't take it out on Volkmann." He started to put his arms around her, then backed away. "I'm just jumpy. Worrying about those hours I can't account for, maybe. Put up with me for a little while longer, okay?"

Karyn gazed at him levelly. "Have you remembered anything more about last night?"

"No, I haven't," he said, the sharpness returning to his voice. "If anything comes to me I'll tell you about it. It doesn't help any to have you nagging at me."

"I wasn't nagging, I was asking."

Roy went angrily back to his papers, muttering something too low for Karyn to hear. She went into the kitchen and made a cup of instant coffee, telling herself she must not lose her temper. When she went back into the living room the front door was open and Roy was gone again.

"Oh, damn, damn, damn," Karyn said aloud. "What am I going to do?"

She looked up at the sound of a car stopping outside. Footsteps crossed the clearing, and Inez Polk appeared in the doorway. With a rush of emotion Karyn ran to her friend and embraced her.

"Oh, Inez, I'm so glad you're here. I need somebody so badly."

Inez patted her gently on the shoulder until Karyn regained her composure and stepped back.

"How did you know to come?"

"Dr. Volkmann called and told me about Roy, and I came as soon as I could. How is he?"

Karyn shook her head. "I wish I knew. He's been irritable all day, pacing around the house like a caged animal. He went out this morning, and he's gone again now. I don't know where he goes."

"Exactly what happened to him last night?"

"I don't know. You saw him after our argument when he went into Drago to pay our bills. He didn't come back the rest of the day or all night. Early the next morning I heard something outside the door, and I found him lying there."

"Was he hurt?"

"Just scratches and bruises, but he couldn't remember anything."

"There was no sign that he'd been attacked?"

"No," Karyn said quickly. "I thought of that too."

Inez frowned thoughtfully. "Karyn, we're going to have to act, you and I."

"What do you mean?"

"Talk to the authorities. Will you come with me to the sheriff's office in Pinyon?"

"I thought we'd decided they wouldn't believe us."

"Not if we told them there's a werewolf here, they wouldn't, but we've got to get them interested somehow. What about those two hikers who stopped here? What were their names?"

"Neal Edwards and Pam Sealander. But I don't see what we can do now."

"Maybe we can get somebody interested enough to start asking questions. At least it's a beginning, and better than just waiting for the next thing to happen."

"Yes, of course it is," Karyn agreed. "I'll leave a note for Roy and be right with you."

Karyn inserted a blank sheet of paper into Roy's typewriter and pecked out: *Dear Roy—I've gone into Pinyon with Inez to do some shopping. I won't be late. Love, Karyn.* She left the note in the typewriter and went out with Inez to get into the car.

They drove down the lane and slowly through the main street of Drago. As usual, there was little activity in the village. A few of the silent people were out on the street. None of them looked up as the women drove past.

Three miles out of Drago, where the road started to climb into the Tehachapi Mountains, Inez turned off on a little-used back road. In a few minutes they reached Pinyon. The contrast to the dark village of Drago was startling. Here flowers bloomed, children laughed, and people smiled at you on the street. It made Drago look like a town in perpetual shadow.

Inez drove to a neat cinderblock building that housed the local sheriff's substation. The women went inside and introduced themselves to the uniformed young man at the desk.

"Good afternoon, ladies," he said pleasantly. "I'm Deputy Paul Spears. What can I do for you?"

"We want to inquire about some missing hikers," said Inez.

"I see." The deputy took a pad from his desk and picked up a ballpoint pen. "What are the people's names?"

"Neal Edwards and Pam—I suppose that's Pamela— Sealander. They have been missing for some time."

Karyn proceeded to tell the entire story, as the deputy took rapid notes.

When she had finished, the deputy looked up. "Are you sure the van you saw belonged to this Edwards and Sealander?"

"I'm reasonably sure. As I said, they told me they were driving a van and they had left it in Drago. When I saw it, it was being hooked up to a tow truck. I went over to ask why. The tow-truck driver told me he had instructions from a man named Anton Gadak."

"Yes, I know Mr. Gadak," the deputy put in. "Since the sheriff's department doesn't patrol Drago, he's been our unofficial contact there."

Karyn's hopes sagged, but she went gamely on. "When I asked Anton Gadak about the van he gave very evasive answers. He didn't seem interested in knowing who owned it. He said there was no registration or identification inside."

"Are you saying that Mr. Gadak was not telling the truth?"

"I think he knows more than he told me."

"I see. And have you any evidence to indicate that these people, as you suggest, met with foul play?"

Karyn's throat closed up, and she could not speak. She looked to Inez for help.

"We have no evidence," Inez said. "There is no proof that anything happened to them. But those two people are unaccounted for, and that should be reason enough to investigate."

"It will be looked into," the deputy assured her. "Now suppose you give me the home addresses of the missing people."

"They're from Santa Barbara," Karyn said. "That's as much as I know."

"We'll check out the names through the police there. If your people are in fact missing, we'll be in touch with you."

"Is that all you're going to do?" Karyn asked.

"Ma'am, excuse me, but this doesn't sound like what

you'd call an emergency. After all, from your account you waited five days before reporting that you were worried about these people."

"I know, but . . . other things have happened since. Couldn't you do something now?"

"What would you suggest?"

Inez took over. "Come with us to Drago and talk to Anton Gadak. He might be more willing to talk to you about the van."

While Deputy Spears considered the request, another young man in a sheriff's-department uniform came into the office.

"Take over the desk for me, will you, Jed?" said Spears. "I'm going over to Drago with these ladies. I shouldn't be gone long." He came around the desk and gestured Karyn and Inez out of the building ahead of him.

While the women buckled themselves into Inez' Valiant, Deputy Spears drove a black-and-white sheriff's car out of the parking lot and pulled up behind them. Inez started down the road toward Drago with the deputy following.

"Do you really think this will do any good?" Karyn asked.

"We can hope," said Inez. "At least it can't do any harm."

Karyn gazed out the window at the trees slipping by. "I only wish I could be sure of that."

CHAPTER
TWENTY-ONE

When the two cars turned up the main street of Drago, Anton Gadak was standing beneath the empty theater marquee, almost as though he had been waiting for them. Under the ever-present Stetson the white bandage still covered his ear.

Inez pulled to the side of the street and stopped. The deputy swung in and parked behind her. Gadak nodded to the women, touching his hat brim, and walked back to the sheriff's car.

"Hi, Paul," he said as the deputy climbed out. "Haven't seen you for a spell."

"They've been keeping me pretty busy," the deputy said.

"What can I do for you?"

Deputy Spears waited for Inez and Karyn to get out of the car and come back to join them. "These two ladies

161

have some questions, Mr. Gadak."

"That so?"

"They're concerned about a couple of people who are missing. Backpackers."

"Yes." Karyn did not look at Anton Gadak. "They parked their van here in town."

"Van?" Gadak rubbed his chin in apparent puzzlement. His callused fingers made a raspy sound.

"It was taken away by a tow truck," Karyn said.

"Oh, sure, the van," Gadak said. "The one you was worried about the other day. That was parked out here on the street for a week. Nobody showed up to claim it, so I called the Highway Patrol to come and get it. That's what we always do with an abandoned vehicle. More'n likely it was stolen by kids and dumped here when they were through with it."

"It wasn't stolen," Karyn said heatedly, "and it wasn't abandoned. It belonged to a boy named Neal Edwards who was hiking up here in the mountains with his girl-friend."

"I wouldn't know anything about that," Gadak said. "Like I told you the other day, there was no registration. The Highway Patrol can check out the owner through the license number. I ain't equipped to do that."

"And it wasn't parked here for any week, either," Karyn persisted.

" 'Scuse me, Mrs. Beatty," Gadak said, "but that vehicle was parked right here in front of this theater for a full seven days. Otherwise, I would've let it be."

Karyn looked at Deputy Spears. She saw he was accepting Gadak's story.

"You can check it out with the Highway Patrol, Paul," Gadak said. "They took the van over to Palmdale. Sergeant Cutter's the man to talk to there."

"I'll give him a call," said the deputy. He turned to Karyn and Inez. "Apparently Mr. Gadak acted here strictly in accordance with our procedures. Did you have any other questions?"

"Is that it?" Karyn said. "Is that all you're going to do?"

"I can check with the Highway Patrol in Palmdale if you want, but it's their job to get in touch with the owner of an impounded vehicle."

"What about Santa Barbara? You said you could do something there."

"All I can do is send a routine request for information to the local police."

"You're brushing us off, aren't you?" Karyn's voice was tight with anger.

Deputy Spears looked down, but failed to hide a patronizing expression.

In frustration, Inez Polk, who had been standing by watching, spoke up. "Mr. Gadak, what happened to your ear?"

Gadak turned on her suddenly, but his expression revealed nothing. He took off the Stetson and touched the bandage.

"You mean this?" he said. "I had a boil back there. It was pretty sore, but I guess it ought to be all right by now. I probably don't even need this bandage any more."

He pulled the strips of adhesive loose and eased the gauze pad away from his head. Underneath was an ear—intact and unmarked.

Gadak's smile was cold. "I appreciate your askin', but as you can see, it's nothing to worry about. Was there anything else I can do for you ladies?"

"No," Karyn said quickly. "Sorry we troubled you."

Deputy Spears politely took his leave, and Karyn and Inez walked back to the Valiant. The women drove away without a glance to the rear, but Karyn knew Anton Gadak's eyes had followed them.

"Why did you do that?" Karyn said. "Come right out and ask him about his ear?"

"I had to do something. It was obvious the deputy wasn't going to help us."

"But what good did it do? All we found out is that Gadak's ear is all right."

"It is now, but remember it's been three days since you shot the wolf. I told you those creatures heal amazingly fast from ordinary wounds."

"But it could have been a boil, as he said."

"Do you believe that?"

"I don't know what to believe."

Inez turned up the narrow road. Suddenly Karyn could hold herself in check no longer. She broke into great wracking sobs that shook her whole body, and couldn't stop. Inez brought the car to a stop and took Karyn in her arms. Karyn responded instantly, pressing herself against her friend.

For the first time in many days Karyn relaxed completely and let the tears come. Her locked-in emotions flooded out as though a gate had been opened. After several minutes the convulsive sobbing eased and she was able to draw a full breath. Still, in her need for another human being, she continued to cling to Inez.

"Is the whole world insane?" she said, her face pressed to Inez' shoulder. "Or are we?"

"Things will work out," Inez said softly. "We mustn't give up."

"You're the only one I have any more," Karyn said. "Roy is so strange lately, I can't even talk to him. Dr. Volkmann seems so removed from things, and Oriole Jolivet, well, she's just Oriole. There's nobody else. I need you, Inez."

Inez stroked Karyn's arm and leaned close. Her lips brushed Karyn's hair. Abruptly, she pulled away.

"I'll take you home now, Karyn."

Karyn straightened in the seat and looked at her friend. "Is something wrong?"

"Nothing is wrong. I have things I must do, that's all."

She put the car in gear and drove on toward the house. Karyn ran a hand over her hair and kept her eyes to the front.

"I'm sorry," Karyn said. "It's thoughtless of me to take up so much of your time."

"No, it's all right," said Inez. "But I really have to go."

She pulled up in front of the little house and Karyn got out. Inez did not meet her eye.

"Well . . . thanks," Karyn said uncertainly. "Will I . . . see you again?"

"Yes, of course. I'll get in touch with you."

Karyn stood in front of the house and watched as Inez backed the car around and drove away. She waved her hand, but there was no sign that Inez had seen.

Inez Polk kept her eyes straight ahead as she drove back out the narrow lane, up through the main street of Drago, and onto the back road that led to Pinyon. Then she pulled off to the side of the road and stopped. She gripped the steering wheel until her knuckles turned white. Her head fell forward.

"Oh, my God," she said in a voice twisted with pain. "I thought that was all behind me."

She could still feel the press of Karyn's soft body against her own. How close she had come to making a terrible mistake.

Irresistibly her thoughts were drawn back through time. Back to the years in the convent when she was known as Sister Adelaide. For the thousandth time she relived the night the young novitiate had come to her room. The girl was in tears, shaking with a fear she could not name. Inez had taken the girl's hand and sat with her on the narrow bed. She had spoken words of comfort and faith while she stroked the girl's smooth white hand. Gradually she became aware of a response in her body. It was a yearning, a need that was utterly foreign to her.

It had seemed the most natural thing in the world to

take the girl into her arms. The girl had come willingly. No, eagerly.

Without consciously making it happen, Inez had found herself lying on the bed with the girl. Naked. The girl touched her and caressed her in ways Inez could not have imagined. The caresses aroused sensations indescribable. Inez' body, her very soul, had caught fire that night. Her reason fled. She wanted only to possess. To be possessed.

It was there in Inez' narrow bed that they had been found. Inez had left the convent and the order immediately and in silence. The girl was turned out, of course. Inez never heard from her again. Never tried to contact her. Tried never to think about her. In vain. For often in an empty night when she lay between chaste sheets in her solitary bed, Inez' hand would stray over her own body and she would remember the delicious, forbidden caresses.

Never since then had she been tempted to act against the laws of God and nature. Never until tonight when she had held Karyn Beatty so briefly in her arms. Inez knew there had been no intent on Karyn's part to arouse her. No response at all in *that* way. If there had been . . . if Karyn had really wanted her . . .

Inez forced herself to break off the thought. She pounded the steering wheel with her fists, letting the pain drive the unwanted memories from her mind. She had to think of other things. She would have a busy day tomorrow doing library research. It would fill her mind. Tonight she would read a very dull book until she fell asleep.

"Please, dear God, don't let me dream."

CHAPTER TWENTY-TWO

Roy Beatty heard Inez' car approaching well before it reached the house. Since the other night when . . . when whatever it was had happened to him in the woods, Roy's hearing, along with his other senses, had become unnaturally keen. He was aware of the change particularly at night. As he lay sleepless beside Karyn he could hear a whole symphony of night sounds that had been inaudible to him before. Tiny forest creatures chittered and squeaked. Trees groaned, their branches clacked and whispered in the dark. The house itself had a score of voices as boards creaked, a shingle flapped, the stone foundation settled another millimeter.

The nights were restless times for Roy. He had acquired an ache in his joints that came when the sun went down and made it difficult for him to find a comfortable position in bed. Knowing how worried Karyn was, he held himself still and pretended to be asleep whenever she looked over at him. All the time his mind was fully alert and ranging far from the bed where he lay.

In the daylight hours his nerves jumped like worms on a griddle. Although he tried, he could not sit still for more than a few minutes. Karyn's presence in the same room irritated him for no reason. Only when he walked in the forest did Roy find partial peace. Striding along through the brush, inhaling the myriad new smells, listening to the daytime forest music—so different from that of the night—Roy knew a kinship with his surroundings. But even at those times he felt incomplete. When he returned home after hours of walking in the woods he would be jumpier than ever.

Roy had tried very hard to remember what had happened to him the night Karyn found him lying outside the door. All he could bring to mind were vague, shifting images. There was some kind of an animal, of that he was sure. And the eyes, always the eyes. Green as jade. Eyes that knew him too well.

But the picture would never form completely, and as his head began to hurt Roy would give up trying.

He heard Inez Polk's car drive away. A minute went by before Karyn came into the house. She was blurry and red around the eyes.

"Oh, you're home," she said.

"Yes. I found your note. Is anything wrong, Karyn? Have you been crying?"

She started to come to him, then something seemed to stop her, hold her back.

"Roy, are you feeling well enough for us to leave?"

"Leave? What do you mean, leave?"

"I want to go away from this place. It's not healthy for you or for me."

"Leave Drago?" Sudden apprehension sent a chill through him.

"The other day you said we would go back to Los Angeles. I'm ready now."

"I don't remember saying that."

"If we don't get out of here something awful will happen to us. I know it—"

Roy stepped toward Karyn and put his arms around her. She was stiff and unresponsive. He released her.

"All right, if you want to go, that settles it. We'll go."

"When?"

"We can't just walk away. It will take time to make arrangements. We'll have to do something about this house. And we sublet our place in the city for a full six months."

"How soon *can* we go?"

"Dammit, I don't know." Roy felt an anger building that was far out of proportion to the cause. He made an effort to be calm. "If you're in such a hurry, why don't you go back alone? I'll come after I get things straightened out."

"I don't want to do that, Roy. I want us to leave together."

"All right," he said, "we'll leave in a week. That will give me time to tie up loose ends here and find somewhere for us to stay in Los Angeles until we can get our apartment back."

"Thank you, darling," Karyn said, greatly relieved.

"Sure." Roy continued to fight down the irrational anger. "Now that it's settled, why don't we have a drink?"

"Are you sure it will be all right for you?"

"Hell yes. There's nothing wrong with me."

"I'll mix them. Are martinis all right?"

"Sure, fine." Roy had not taken a drink since his experience in the woods. He had no desire for alcohol now. But having a drink had seemed like a good way to get off the subject of leaving Drago. The raw smell of gin burned his nostrils as Karyn stirred the cocktails out in the kitchen.

She brought in two icy glasses and handed one to Roy. He took a sip, swallowed, and the liquor tore at his throat like broken glass. He fell into a coughing spasm.

Karyn, quickly putting down her own glass, came to his side. "Are you all right?"

It took several seconds for Roy to get his breath back to answer. "Some of it went down the wrong way, I guess."

"Maybe you shouldn't drink on an empty stomach."

Roy sniffed at the glass in his hand and his stomach turned over. "Maybe you're right." He set the glass down and moved away from it, trying to mask the overpowering revulsion he felt.

"I'll start dinner," Karyn said. "What would you like to eat?"

"It doesn't matter. The truth is I'm not very hungry."

"You really should eat something. You've barely touched your food the last two days."

"Cut it out, will you? You're starting to sound like a Jewish mother."

What Roy could not tell his wife was that he *did* have a hunger. A bone-deep gnawing need for something, he didn't know what.

"I only asked what you wanted for dinner," she said.

"I don't give a damn," he snapped. "Cook anything you want to."

Karyn looked up at him quickly. The hurt in her eyes made him want to reach out for her, but he could not. She turned away and went into the kitchen.

For their dinner she prepared pork chops with baked potatoes, creamed carrots, and a green salad. Roy barely picked at the vegetables. He knew his stomach would not accept them.

"Is something wrong with the food?" Karyn asked.

"It's fine. Too bad you burned the pork chops, though."

"They aren't burned, Roy. They're done the way I always do them."

"Then you always burn them."

Karyn chose her words carefully. "You have to cook pork well. You know that, Roy."

He slapped his napkin down and left the table. "I don't want to argue about any stupid pork chops."

For the rest of the evening Roy pretended to work while Karyn pretended to read. At last it was time to go to bed. Roy got in next to his wife and lay rigidly still, not wanting to touch her, praying that she would not touch him. The aching in his joints was the worst yet. After a very long time Karyn's breathing eased, her features softened. She was asleep.

Roy relaxed. Through a gap in the window curtain he could see the moon. He could not remember ever seeing it so bright. The light of it kept his eyes open and made sleep impossible. He got out of bed and walked over to the window. He meant to close the curtain, but when he looked out he was stunned by the beauty of the scene. The full moon suffused the forest with a pale silver light that made everything magical. Roy could not stay inside on a night like this. He gathered his clothes and carried them silently into the living room. There he dressed rapidly and went out.

He plunged at once into the deep shadows of the forest, but had no trouble seeing the path. The combination of bright moonlight and his improved night vision made the going easy. He inhaled and savored the tangy scent of the evergreens. The air was deliciously cool. Roy felt he was embraced by the night.

The tiny things that lived in the darkness—the rodents and the night birds—froze in the shadows as Roy approached. But he saw them and smiled. He was a part of their world.

The cramps in his joints grew suddenly worse. Roy slowed down and rubbed at his shoulders. There was a twisting ache in both his knees. He stumbled into a clearing, and the pain was too great for him to go on.

He recognized the clearing. It was the place where he had come upon Marcia Lura the night he had gone looking for Karyn's wolf. It seemed so very long ago, yet it was less than a week.

Breathing became difficult. Roy tore at his collar. It was loose at the throat, yet it choked him like a noose. He pulled the shirt open all the way down the front and peeled it from his back. Better. The cool night kissed his flesh. He eased into a sitting position and pulled off his shoes and socks. The grass was like velvet against his bare feet. The cloth of his pants rasped against his skin, and he pulled them off too. Roy pulled himself erect, naked in the clearing. He bathed in the clean night air.

Then a violent muscular spasm seized him and he lost control of his body. He dropped to the ground, his hands braced out in front of him. As Roy stared at his hands a growth of short yellowish hair spread over the backs. The fingers shortened and grew claws. The palms thickened into pads, and the hands were paws. Simultaneously, thick pale fur covered his body, his arms and legs twisted into new shapes, his ears grew points, his face lengthened into a muzzle. He flicked his tongue over the new cruel fangs in his mouth.

As his body changed, so did the mind of Roy Beatty. The logical, rational, well-ordered human consciousness was crowded into a far corner of the new intelligence. The mind that now controlled the body was wild and cunning. The mind knew—Roy Beatty knew—what had happened to him. He had become a wolf.

Tentatively at first, then with growing confidence, he tested the new body. He marveled at the way the four legs worked in effortless rhythm, bearing him swiftly over the ground. He turned his head to look down along the thickly furred back. He could see the long muscles moving smoothly under his pelt. And there was the fine thick tail that provided balance for this graceful creature he had become. The delight he felt at his transformation was beyond anything in Roy Beatty's experience. There were no words for it in the human vocabulary. He wheeled once around the perimeter of the clearing, then bounded off into the darkness of the forest.

He disdained the paths, moving easily through narrow openings in the underbrush. The powerful legs carried him swiftly along, the keen eyes and nose following faint animal trails. On he plunged, growing careless of the protruding twigs and branches as he discovered his body was protected by the thick covering of fur.

As he crashed through the undergrowth the big pale wolf became aware of hungers that squeezed his belly like a giant's hand. The craving was for food and drink, and other things. The need was powerful, but the spark of human intelligence that remained still fought it.

The wolf loped on. The satisfying stretch and pull of his muscles filled the consciousness of the beast and, at least for a while, kept out the dreadful hungers.

Then in mid-bound the wolf tensed and jammed to a stop. A sound from far away in the forest stabbed into the animal's brain. He froze, slowly turning the great head this way and that, sampling the air, listening.

The sound came again. A high-pitched wail of unearthly beauty. The howling. It spoke to the pale wolf, called to him. No steel-jawed trap could have kept the pale wolf that night from the one that howled.

The beast raised his muzzle to the night sky and gave his own answering call. Then with an unerring sense of direction he wheeled and ran back through the night.

It was in the same clearing where Roy Beatty had left his clothes that the pale wolf found her. A lithe she-wolf with sleek fur blacker than the shadows of the night. Her eyes reflected the pale moon in twin green sparks. Her lips drew back from the sharp strong teeth and the she-wolf gave a soft, taunting growl.

The nostrils of the pale wolf distended, filled with the wild, musky scent of the female. He stopped in front of her, feet braced wide, neck fur bristling, and gave an answering growl, low and harsh. The she-wolf switched her tail and moved away from him in slow, sidling steps.

He sprang at her, but the wolf bitch leaped nimbly aside and he came down on empty grass. The green eyes of the female burned into the darker eyes of the male. Roy Beatty the man had never known such overwhelming lust as now consumed the pale wolf. Again he lunged for the bitch, and again she sidestepped just enough to elude him.

The animal mind of the pale wolf understood the game then. He feinted another leap and the she-wolf moved to one side. Instantly he changed direction and sprang upon her. Their legs became entangled and they rolled together on the grassy carpet of the clearing. Their flashing teeth caught each other wherever there was loose flesh. They bit hard enough to hurt, but not to injure.

Abruptly the she-wolf broke off the mock battle and moved a short distance away. She turned and looked over her shoulder, offering herself to him. The pale wolf was on her in an instant, and took her with cruel animal haste. The climax was sudden and explosive. For a moment the two wolves stood locked together. Then the bitch pulled free and sank to her side. The male wolf dropped beside her, his tongue lolling, his ribcage working like a bellows.

At last they both lay quiet. The male told in soft growls and whines of the other hunger that was still unsatisfied. The female answered him in murmurs that said, *Soon.*

As the moon sank behind a ridge of mountains, the black she-wolf rose suddenly and slipped into the forest. Without a sound she was gone. The big pale wolf got unsteadily to his feet. The animal mind was becoming confused. Images faded and broke up, human and bestial thoughts intermingled.

The wolf's muscles twitched and jerked convulsively.

Its eyes rolled wildly. With its graceful movements turned awkward, the wolf staggered toward the untidy pile of Roy Beatty's clothes.

CHAPTER TWENTY-THREE

The black night sky was smudged with charcoal at the eastern rim of mountains when Roy Beatty came back to the house. He let himself in and walked straight to the bedroom. In the bed Karyn slept uneasily. Or pretended to sleep. To Roy it made no difference now.

He was deadly tired, but he did not want to get into the bed without bathing. He had to get the dirt of the forest off him. And the smell of the she-wolf.

He cleansed himself under the shower and came back into the bedroom, not even bothering to be quiet. Karyn's eyes were open, staring at the ceiling. She did not speak. Roy crawled in beside her and dropped instantly into a dreamless sleep.

He slept the day through. When he finally awoke in the evening, his mind was clear, but oddly out of synchronization. Karyn was in the living room when he went out. She made no attempt to speak to him, for which he was thankful. He wanted no intimacies now, physical or verbal, with his wife.

As it grew darker outside the night called to him. He fought against the call as best he could. The portion of his mind that was still Roy Beatty cried out its warning, but its voice was small and far away. Still he made an effort. He built the fire high and sat before it shivering as he fought to stay where he was. And what he was.

Perspiration soaked through his clothes. Every bone in his body ached. The night forest called out to him, and finally it would not be denied. He could not even wait until Karyn was in bed. The hunger was in him and there was no resisting.

He sprang to his feet. He looked at Karyn, and for a brief second his face mirrored the agony of his soul. Then he ran out the door and was lost in the night.

Inez Polk sat alone in her tidy little house in Pinyon. She was surrounded by her books of werewolf lore and the yellowed clippings she had saved for years. The glasses kept slipping down her long thin nose as she bent over the maple desk.

In the two days since she had driven away from Karyn Beatty, Inez had kept herself constantly busy. At school she had volunteered to take the classes of a sixth-grade teacher who was ill. At home she had read over and over these volumes that she already knew so well.

At first her purpose had been self-prescribed therapy to keep her from thinking about Karyn, about what almost happened to her. By total concentration on her reading and note-taking, she had been able to fall exhausted into bed sometime after midnight the night before.

Tonight, however, as she carefully read and reread the several versions of the legend of Dradja, something began to tug at her mind. Thoughts of sleep were forgotten as the adrenalin of discovery began to flow.

The people of the old village of Dradja, even when subjected to unspeakable tortures, refused to give up one of their number to the mob.

Why?

Again and again Inez read the words before her. Like a cold draft from an open winter window the truth swept upon her. She knew at last the secret of Dradja. And the secret of Drago.

"God forgive me," she said aloud. "We were such fools to ask, 'Who in the village is the werewolf?' "

Without bothering to put her books away, Inez hurried to the closet to get her coat. She rushed out of the house and got into her car, firing the engine with an impatient twist of the key. If she was too late . . . if anything had happened to Karyn . . .

Inez did not let herself complete the thought. She gave her full concentration to driving. Soon the lights of Pinyon were behind her and she was on the road leading to Drago.

Overhead, ragged clouds slid across the moon. The night was alive with shadows. Just beyond the swash of light from the headlamps a hundred pairs of eyes seemed to watch. Inez gripped the wheel harder and drove grimly on.

The main street of Drago was empty and dark. Inez slowed the car as she neared Karyn's turnoff. At the entrance to the rutted lane she braked and turned off the blacktop. She had gone only a few yards when the headlights picked out something moving at the side of the road up ahead. Inez tensed as the cold hand of fear came down on her back. The brush parted and a figure stepped out into the road. A man. He raised his hands toward the oncoming car, commanding her to stop.

"No you don't," Inez said through clenched teeth. "You will not stop me."

She drove on. The man in the road did not move.

"I'll run you down," she said aloud. "I know what you

are, and I'll run you down before I let you at me."

The muscles of her arms corded with the effort of holding the wheel straight. She steeled herself for the coming impact. At the last moment she recognized the man standing in front of her, and hit the brake pedal.

Roy Beatty.

The car lurched to a stop not an arm's length from Roy, who stood his ground without flinching. Inez let her head sag forward against the steering wheel. For a moment she was faint with relief. Now she was not alone.

Then she realized there must be something wrong at the house for Roy to be standing out here. She reached across to unlock the door on the passenger's side. Not until the door started to swing open did she realize that the face outside in the dark was not Roy Beatty's. It was not the face of any human being.

Inez Polk screamed just once, then the beast ripped out her throat. There was hardly any pain, just a bubbling sensation of drowning in something hot, and then it was over.

The engine of the Valiant continued to idle softly. The only other sound was the crunch of bone as the pale wolf fed its hunger.

CHAPTER
TWENTY-FOUR

~~~~~~

Karyn lay on her side with her back to Roy. This was the second night he had slipped out of the house late and not returned until sometime before dawn. Unanswered questions tumbled through Karyn's mind, but she could not find the voice to ask them.

Although they were not touching, Karyn felt a strangeness about Roy's body as he lay next to her. A subtle difference that she sensed rather than saw. Ever since the morning she had found him lying outside the door something had been working on him. In these few days a stranger had moved in and taken the place of her husband.

Roy had always been a gentle man, understanding and compassionate. Now, Karyn sensed a roiling violence that might erupt at any time.

He was sleeping now. A heavy, unmoving sleep. Karyn

raised up in the bed to look at him. It was the same square, innocent face, the same pale-blond hair and light powdery eyelashes. The broad chest and the powerful shoulders, bare now above the sheet, were unchanged. And yet . . . there was *something*. Even asleep, the man had an aura of danger.

Karyn lay back down on her side of the bed and stared at the window. She had to leave this place without delay. With Roy if he would agree to go, without him otherwise. One way or another she had to get away from here.

If Roy was difficult, she would need help from someone else. A friend. Oriole? Dr. Volkmann? No, they were too much a part of Drago. She could never explain to them why.

Inez Polk. Inez knew what was happening here. She would help. If nothing else, Karyn could stay with her in Pinyon until it could be arranged for someone to come from Los Angeles. With the decision made, Karyn relaxed. She moved well away from the inert form of her husband and, as the dawn broke, lapsed into a shallow sleep.

When they got up later in the morning Roy was full of energy. His face had lost its pale look of recent days and had a ruddy glow. He was in high spirits. Too high. Almost manic.

He threw open the window and stood naked before it, breathing deeply. "Just smell that air. Better than wine."

Karyn watched him carefully. "What shall we have for breakfast?"

"You have whatever you want. I don't need any breakfast. The beautiful day is my breakfast. The trees, the sky, the song of the birds."

Karyn tried to smile. "That's very poetic, but not awfully nourishing. Seriously, what would you like to eat?"

Without warning his mood darkened. "Nothing. Isn't that what I said? I'm not hungry."

"Roy, we've got to talk."

"Go ahead, I'm listening."

"This place is destroying us."

"That's ridiculous. I never felt better."

"You said we would leave Drago in a week."

"Did I?"

"Yes, you did. But I don't think a week is soon enough."

"What's the matter? There's no great hurry, is there?"

"I think there is. I want us to go now."

He turned to face her squarely. "That sounds like an order."

"I can't help what it sounds like. I will not stay in this valley any longer."

"What if I refuse to go?"

Karyn caught her breath, but answered in a clear, firm voice. "In that case, Roy, I'll go without you."

A shadow of hurt darkened his eyes for just an instant.

"This is not some crazy whim," Karyn went on. "I have good reasons—"

"I don't want to hear your reasons," Roy spat out. "If you're going to come at me with orders and ultimatums, you can forget it." His face hardened into a mask Karyn did not know.

"I'm going to town," she said. She turned and went out the door without waiting for a response.

The trees moved restlessly on both sides of the narrow road. A hot desert wind was blowing, funneled into the valley through a gap in the mountains to the east. The walk to town seemed much shorter than the first time she had tried it. If nothing else, the stay in Drago had made her physically stronger.

Oriole Jolivet hurried out to meet her as she entered the store. "Hey, Karyn, did you hear what happened?"

"Can it keep for a minute, Oriole? I have an important phone call I have to make."

"Well, sure, help yourself."

Oriole's hurt feelings could be soothed later. Karyn picked up the phone and dialed Inez Polk's number in

Pinyon. This was Friday, and Inez had classes only in the afternoon.

The receiver buzzed in her ear as the phone rang on the other end. Karyn waited for the five rings she usually allowed, then five more. No answer. Maybe Inez had gone to school early. Karyn hung up.

"Nobody home?" Oriole asked.

"Apparently not."

Karyn leafed through the telephone book, looking for the number of the school.

"You weren't tryin' to call that friend of yours from over in Pinyon, that Inez, were you?"

Something in Oriole's voice gave Karyn a chill. "Yes."

"Then you haven't heard." Oriole bit her lower lip and shook her head sadly.

"Heard what?"

"She was killed last night."

"Killed?" Karyn felt as though she had been punched in the stomach.

"Ran her car smack into a tree. It happened on the turnoff up by your place. Looks like she might have been on her way to see you."

"A car accident?" Karyn's mind wanted to reject the words. "How did it happen?"

"Hard to say. Anton Gadak thinks she must have dozed off at the wheel. It was him found her about six o'clock this morning."

It would be Anton Gadak. "Was she dead when he found her?"

"Yep. Looked like she died instantly, Anton says."

"Where did they take her?"

"The hospital over in Pinyon, but I don't think you want to go see her. She was cut up awful bad, Anton says. Must have gone through the windshield."

Not with her seat belt fastened, and Inez' car would not start without it. Karyn closed her eyes for a moment, realizing the full horror of the situation. Inez must have learned something and have been coming to tell her about it. The only thing that would have brought her over late at night was the identity of the Drago werewolf. Somehow the beast had got her.

Oriole came over and laid a pudgy hand on Karyn's shoulder. "I'm awful sorry, Karyn. It really hits a person when a friend dies. At least it happened fast. I knew a woman once . . ."

Oriole's voice droned on, but her words faded from Karyn's mind. First Roy, now Inez. One by one she was losing the few people she could call on for help. Who was left? A name jumped into her thoughts. Chris Halloran. She had forced herself not to think about Chris since the day she had so cruelly sent him away. She had thought vaguely that she would make it up to him someday. Now she had no time.

She wondered if Chris would even speak to her after her hysterical performance. But he was all she had left.

". . . know how you feel, Karyn, but these things happen. Like they say, life goes on." Oriole's voice came back into her consciousness.

"Is it all right if I make a long-distance call?" Karyn said. "I'll ask the operator how much it is and pay you for it."

"Sure it's all right. Who you calling?"

"A friend. In Los Angeles."

Oriole stood her ground until Karyn made it clear by standing with her hand on the receiver that she was not going to place the call until she was left alone.

"I'll, uh, go attend to some things in the back," Oriole said.

Karyn nodded. It was too late to bother with the niceties of courtesy. When Oriole had gone she asked for the Los Angeles information operator and got from her the number of Chris's company, Western Industrial Design. She dialed the number, and a woman's voice answered with the name of the firm.

"I'd like to speak to Mr. Halloran."

"Mr. Halloran didn't come in today. Can someone else help you?"

"Do you happen to have his home phone number?"

"I'm not sure I should—"

"It's all right, I'm Mrs. Roy Beatty. My husband and I are personal friends of Mr. Halloran."

"Oh, yes, Mrs. Beatty, I've heard him mention your name. Hold on a second, I'll get the number for you."

As Karyn waited, Etienne Jolivet came in the front of the store. He nodded to her solemnly.

"Is that you, Etienne?" Oriole called from the back. "Can you come out here a minute?"

The tall man moved silently past the counter and through the door into the back room.

The girl came back on the line and gave Karyn Chris Halloran's home telephone number. Karyn memorized it, thanked the girl, and hung up. She called the operator back and asked the charges for the call. It came to $1.19. She noted the sum on the back of a brown paper bag and picked up the phone again. She dialed the Los Angeles area code and Chris's home number.

Be there, she thought. *Oh, please, God, let him be there*. The receiver buzzed in her ear. Halfway through the second buzz there was a click. Karyn went weak with sudden relief. She opened her mouth to say hello, but before she could frame a greeting, Chris's voice came on the line.

"Hi, this is Chris Halloran. Sorry I'm not home at the moment. What you're hearing is my answering machine. If you'll wait for the beep, then leave any message and your number, I'll get back to you as soon as I can."

Karyn wanted to sob in frustration as another hope flickered out. She started to lower the receiver back into the cradle; then the electronic tone beeped faintly. There was still the possibility that Chris was just out of the apartment for a moment. It would be foolish for her to have come this far and not even leave a message.

What could she say? How much time did these things allow for a message? Sixty seconds? Thirty? In as calm a voice as she could manage, Karyn began to speak.

"Chris, this is Karyn Beatty. I'm in trouble, and I need your help. If you hear this, please come to Drago for me. And, Chris, bring a gun."

She hesitated, knowing how crazy the rest of it would sound. She forced herself to go on. "Load the gun with silver bullets if you can. There isn't time to explain anything now, but please, oh please, Chris, believe I need you."

Gently she replaced the instrument and stood for several seconds staring down at it, wondering what effect her words would have on Chris Halloran. Wondering if he would even hear them in time.

"All through with your phone calls?"

Karyn started, then put on a smile as Oriole Jolivet came up beside her.

"Yes, I am. I'll just find out how much it was." She dialed the operator and was told that the charge was another $1.19.

"The total comes to $2.38," she told Oriole. She dipped into her change purse for two dollar bills, a quarter, dime, and nickel.

"I'll owe you the two cents," Oriole said.

"I guess I can trust you for it." Karyn tried to smile, but her face felt all wrong.

Oriole regarded her soberly. "Listen, Karyn, if there's anything I can do, anything at all, just say the word. People sometimes think I'm just a fat, silly woman. I'm more than that."

"I know you are, Oriole," Karyn said softly.

"And maybe I'm not an old friend, but I can be a good one if you'll let me. You know where to find me. You tell Roy hello for me, now, and come on back when you feel like playin' some gin."

"I will," Karyn said. "And thank you, Oriole. Goodbye."

She went out of the store, and the hot desert wind pushed against her as she walked up the street. The dry heat sucked away the moisture of her skin, leaving it feeling scaly. In Los Angeles they called it the Santa Ana wind. They said it made people a little bit mad.

In the shadow of a doorway on the far side of the street—*always in the shadow*—stood Anton Gadak. His eyes were invisible under the brim of the Stetson. Karyn looked away quickly and hurried on.

When she reached the turnoff to the road that led to her house, Karyn stopped and looked around. There was no tree anywhere near the road that was big enough to smash a car. Whatever had killed Inez Polk, Karyn was sure it was not an accident.

A short distance up the narrow lane, something glittered on the ground. Karyn bent down to look, and recognized the metal frame, now twisted, and thick lenses of Inez' glasses. She slipped the ruined glasses into her pocket and started home again when something else caught her eye. At the side of the road, partly hidden by the brush, was a tennis shoe. A worn Adidas, white with blue stripes. Roy had a pair like that.

Karyn shuddered, despite the hot wind, and turned away. She walked on rapidly toward the house. In a very few hours it would be dark.

CHAPTER
TWENTY-FIVE

~~~~~~

Chris Halloran's hopes of getting away early for a weekend of loafing in Ensenada were fading fast. He had planned to hit the border by midmorning, but here it was afternoon and he hadn't left yet. His mistake had been to drop in on one of the clients of his engineering firm to see how a new tool-design concept was working out. There were problems. Nothing serious, but as long as Chris was on the scene he could hardly refuse to have a look. By the time he finished, it was two o'clock.

On the way home he had made one more stop at a drugstore to pick up a few small items for his traveling bag. He waited impatiently in the checkout line while everyone ahead of him, it seemed, had to cash a check written on a Hong Kong bank.

At last he pulled into the underground parking area of

the Surf King Apartments. The image conjured by the name had always amused Chris. Blond young giants in deep tans and cutoffs hanging ten as they hotdogged in with the heavies. Actually, the average age of Surf King tenants was comfortably over thirty, and there weren't half a dozen of them who could stand up on a surfboard. The whole marina scene was beginning to pall on Chris. The same funky-chic people in the same overpriced bars on Friday nights, telling the same lies over the same drinks and looking for . . . what?

Chris shook the thought away. He was not by nature a moody young man, and he did not much like himself when he became gloomy. That was the main reason for spending a weekend in Baja. He would go down by himself, get a small, comfortable hotel room, drink a little tequila, maybe do a little fishing. Or maybe just loaf. He liked to walk among the local people on streets where the tourists didn't go. He smiled in anticipation of tortillas hot from the fire and beans and Mexican chilis washed down with icy Carta Blanca. A weekend in Ensenada had always been effective therapy for Chris. He was in a hurry to be on his way.

Back in his airy two-level apartment Chris quickly packed his one small travel bag. He pulled on a comfortable old suede jacket and headed for the door. He stopped before going out to take a last look around. This was the day the cleaning lady came, so everything was shipshape—the big mirror polished, the ash trays gleaming, magazines fanned on the coffee table, cushions geometrically arranged on the three-piece sectional sofa. Chris walked over and pushed the magazines into an untidy stack. When he came back he did not want to feel he was walking into a setting for *Home* magazine.

He started out the door again, but once more he hesitated. Should he play back the morning telephone calls? What if there was one from his office with some problem or other that would mean further delay? He could ignore

the message, of course, but it would bother him all the
time he was in Baja. If he never heard the message, he
wouldn't feel guilty. And who else but the office would
call on a Friday morning?

No, he could not ignore it. Now that the thought had
occurred to him, he would have to play the tape. It
shouldn't take long, and then he could leave with a clear
conscience. He walked back into the apartment, dropped
onto one end of the sofa, and switched on the machine to
play back the taped telephone calls.

The beep sounded, there was a short silence, then a
male voice said, "Oh, the hell with it." A hollow click
followed, and the rest of the allotted thirty seconds was
dial tone. Many people, Chris had found, refused to talk
to a machine. He didn't much blame them.

The machine beeped again. Karyn Beatty's voice came
over the tiny speaker, and Chris sat suddenly upright. He
was so surprised to hear her voice that the first time
through the message did not fully register. Something
about being in trouble and a gun and silver bullets. He
recycled the tape and played it through a second time,
listening carefully.

It was not a joke. There was no mistaking the urgency
in Karyn's voice, and she was not the type to play this
kind of a joke, anyway. But the message . . . *Load the
gun with silver bullets* . . . It was crazy.

Chris played back the thirty seconds of Karyn a third
time, trying to pick up any kind of clue or hidden mean-
ing. As far as he could tell, there was none. He had to
assume that she meant exactly what she said. But, *silver
bullets?*

He played out the rest of the tape to see if there was
anything more from Karyn, but the only other call was a
reminder from his dentist to come in for a checkup.

Chris snapped off the machine and sat for a moment
frowning in thought. He would go at once to Drago, of
course. It was possible that Karyn was imagining some

kind of peril—she had certainly acted irrationally the last time he had seen her—but something in the way she spoke told him the danger was real.

His first impulse was to call the police. But what would he tell them? "My friend's wife is in a little town called Drago and she needs help and says to bring silver bullets." It didn't take much imagination to picture some desk sergeant's response to that. And Karyn must have reasons, or she would have called the authorities herself. He would have to go on his own.

Bring a gun. That would be no problem since he did own one—a .22-caliber Stoeger automatic patterned after the old German Luger. He had bought it a couple of years before for plinking at cans in the desert, and had not fired it since. It was not a weapon that would knock down a moose, but there was no time to get anything bigger. It would have to do.

But silver bullets? Where the hell did you go to get silver bullets?

He had to start somewhere, so he grabbed the fat Los Angeles Yellow Pages and riffled through to *Silversmiths.* He called the firm with the most impressive ad.

A young man's voice answered. "Glendenning Silver, good afternoon."

"Hello," Chris said, feeling foolish, but trying to sound businesslike. "I wonder if you do anything in the way of making bullets?"

"You said bullets?"

"That's what I said. Bullets."

"I think what you want is jewelry. We deal primarily in silverware and plating."

"I don't mean jewelry bullets, I mean real bullets. Real silver bullets."

"Perhaps you'd like to speak to our manager, Mr. Roth."

"I don't have time to play games with your manager.

All I want to know is, can you or can you not make me silver bullets?"

The young man's voice went cold. "We do *not* make bullets, not gold, not silver, not any kind."

Chris slammed down the phone and swore at it. All right, silversmiths do not make bullets. Who does make bullets? Try a gunsmith. Back to the Yellow Pages. Chris picked out the K & K Gun Shop. Their ad featured a businesslike revolver and stated that their services included ammunition and reloading. He dialed the number.

"Yeah?" a gritty voice answered.

"K & K Gun Shop?"

"Yeah."

Might as well get right to it, Chris decided. "Can you make me some silver bullets?"

"You mean bullets made out of silver?"

Stay calm. "That's what I mean."

"Sure."

Chris stared at the phone. As easy as that.

"Bring your own silver. I don't stock that. Naturally."

"I'll bring the silver," Chris said. "Let's see, you're located at . . ." He read off the Vermont Avenue address from the advertisement.

"Yeah. I close at six, so if you're comin' in today you better hurry it up."

"Yes, it has to be today." Chris checked his watch. Jesus, could it be after four already? "I'll try to make it by six, but wait for me if I'm a little late, will you? I'll pay you for any overtime."

"This ain't a joke, is it?"

"It's no joke."

"Okay, but be here as soon as you can."

"I will."

Chris hung up and turned quickly back to the Yellow Pages.

Silver Bullion—See Coin Dlrs. 547

He flipped the pages quickly and found the Excelsior

Coin Co., Gold—Silver—Platinum Coins & Bars Bought & Sold. The address was on Venice Boulevard in Culver City. There was no need to bother with another telephone call. He could save the time by heading straight over there.

Chris started out the door on the run, then snapped his fingers and turned back. He went into the bedroom and reached up to the high closet shelf for the Stoeger .22. He checked the magazine and chamber to be sure it was empty, then pulled the trigger to test the action. The pistol gave a sharp, satisfying click. He dropped it into a jacket pocket and hurried out to his car.

It was twenty minutes to five when he pulled into the lot beside the Excelsior Coin Company. The sun was low in the west and turning an angry red. Chris jumped from the car and ran into the building. A clerk looked at him in surprise from behind the counter.

"I want to buy some silver," Chris said.

"Yes, sir. Coins or bars?"

"Bars, I think."

"In what quantity?"

"What sizes do they come in?"

"Most of our bullion transactions are in five-ounce and ten-ounce bars. For anything larger we'd have to—"

"Those should be large enough. Can I see what they look like?"

"Certainly." The clerk stepped to the rear of the store and returned in a minute with two ingots of pure silver in the shape of tiny Hershey bars.

Chris hefted them, one in each hand. How much silver did it take to make a bullet? He said, "How much for the ten-ounce bar?"

"A single bar is sixty dollars, but if you intend to purchase in volume—"

"One will be enough."

Chris walked over to the cash register to discourage further conversation. He paid for the ingot with his Master

Charge card and took it back out to the car.

The Santa Monica Freeway was clotted with rush-hour traffic. Chris pounded the steering wheel in frustration as all lanes jerked along in an angry dance of flashing tail lights.

The sky was dark when Chris finally turned off the freeway at the Vermont Avenue exit. The surface street traffic was lighter, and he reached the K & K Gun Shop in a few minutes.

The inside of the shop smelled of cosmoline, wood polish, and leather. The walls were lined with rifles and shotguns. In a heavy glass case were handguns ranging from tiny Derringers to a cannon-sized .44 magnum. In the back of the shop a chunky man in a T-shirt worked a piece of metal on a lathe.

"Hello," Chris said. "I called you earlier."

The man turned off the lathe and looked up. "Oh, yeah, the silver bullets."

"That's it."

The gunsmith came around the counter and locked the front door. "Might as well close up," he said. "Won't be no more customers tonight." He pulled an expanding steel lattice across the show window and locked it into place. "Hell of a neighborhood for a gun shop. Did you bring the silver?"

Chris fished the ingot out of his pocket.

"Uh-huh. What caliber bullets you want?"

Chris showed him the Stoeger. "To fit this."

"Twenty-two Long Rifle," said the gunsmith. "How many?"

Chris had not thought about it. The magazine of the Stoeger held eleven. And one in the chamber. Surely that would be enough.

"Twelve," he said.

"Jeez, you brought enough metal."

"Well, use whatever you need."

"Come on in the back."

Chris followed the gunsmith into the workroom and watched as he shaved off what looked like very little of the silver bar and put the shavings in a crucible.

"Is that enough?" Chris asked.

"Hell, yes. A .22 Long Rifle slug only weighs forty grains."

"Oh."

The gunsmith placed the crucible over a gas flame and turned to a shelf behind him to select a mold.

"How hot does it have to get to melt the silver?" Chris asked.

"Nine hundred and sixty point five degrees Centigrade," the man said without turning around.

"You know that by heart?"

The man turned to face him. "Look, buddy, I didn't go to no fancy college and I don't read a whole lot of books, but guns and ammunition are my business. I'd be a piss-poor gunsmith if I didn't know the melting point of metals."

"Hey, no offense," Chris said. "I'm impressed, that's all."

The gunsmith relaxed into a grin. "Don't mind me, I've had a long week." He stuck out a big hand. "My name's Buzz Klinger. Call me Buzz."

Chris took the offered hand. "Glad to know you, Buzz. I'm Chris Halloran."

Klinger returned to his work and went about it with the smooth economy of motion that comes with true crafts-manship. Chris stayed out of the way and watched. When the silver shavings had melted, Klinger poured the molten metal into the molds, filling twelve of them exactly.

"You want regular load or high-power in the cart-ridges?"

"Better make it high-power." It occurred to Chris that Buzz Klinger had not asked what he wanted with silver bullets. His respect for the man increased.

When the silver had cooled in the molds, Klinger

mated the twelve slugs to the loaded cartridges and handed them to Chris along with the unused portion of the silver ingot.

"What do I owe you?" Chris said.

"Ten bucks will cover it."

"How about your overtime?"

"I figured that in already."

Chris peeled off a bill and handed it to Klinger. "Thanks, Buzz. It was a pleasure watching you work."

Klinger unlocked the front door and Chris started out.

"Hey," the gunsmith called as Chris started down the sidewalk.

Chris turned back.

"Give my regards to Tonto."

CHAPTER
TWENTY-SIX

The little house was empty when Karyn returned after her call to Chris Halloran. In a way, she thought, it was just as well that Roy was not there. He had been so strange lately, that it was difficult for her to be around him. The prospect of being alone tonight was not pleasant, but it would be the last night she would spend in Drago.

She locked the front and back doors and all the windows, making sure the heavy screens on the outside were secure. While she was in the bedroom, Karyn went to the closet and looked through the pairs of shoes, hers and Roys, on the floor. She found one of Roy's white-and-blue Adidas. Just one. No time to dwell on the implications of that now. Roy would have an explanation when he came home.

Moving to the hall closet, she took out the shotgun. She loaded the weapon and propped it up beside the front door. Against the thing she feared was out there, the shotgun was almost useless, but it was better than nothing.

Karyn sat down and directed her thoughts to Chris Halloran. Would he come for her? She tried to remember exactly what she had said into the recorder, but the words would not come back. She could only hope that it would not sound too crazy when Chris played it back.

If he played it back. Karyn knew she could not count on Chris or anyone else to help her tonight. She had only herself.

With a suddenness that shocked her, the sun dropped behind the mountains and darkness claimed the valley. Karyn turned on every light in the house. She flicked the switch for the outdoor light that illuminated the clearing in front. Nothing happened. A hell of a time, she thought, for the bulb to burn out. She took a good bulb from one of the lamps and opened the door to put it in the outside fixture. Then she saw it was not a burned-out bulb. The old bulb had been smashed, and the metal socket battered out of shape, making it impossible to screw in another bulb. Karyn slammed the door and leaned against it, breathing hard. After a minute she returned the good bulb to the lamp and lit a fire in the fireplace.

The blank windows, with nothing but the night outside, seemed to Karyn like inward-staring opaque eyes. She drew curtains over the glass.

She went into the kitchen and put on a pot of coffee, making it twice as strong as she usually did. There would be no sleep tonight. On the counter she found a carton of Roy's cigarettes. She lit one and pulled in the smoke hungrily.

Soon Karyn found she could not stand it with the curtains closed. Her imagination populated the night with worse horrors than could possibly be there. The moon had come out, so at least she could see a little in the front of the house. The desert wind had not subsided at nightfall, and the boughs of the surrounding trees moved restlessly.

To keep her mind active Karyn thought about what she would do the next day. Whether Roy came back or not, one way or another she would leave this cursed town. Consider the possibilities. Call from Drago for a taxi to come in from Los Angeles and get her, and damn the expense. If an L.A. taxi would not make the trip, try Pinyon. They must have some sort of taxi service there.

If she couldn't get a taxi, she would go out on the road and hitchhike. Take the first ride offered in either direction just to get away from Drago.

If there were no other way, she would take Roy's car and somehow drive the damn thing. She only had to go far enough to get away from Drago. And what did it matter if she damaged the car? It would be a small price to pay for escape.

Satisfied with this plan, Karyn went into the bedroom and searched through Roy's things until she found the spare set of keys. She tucked them into a pocket and felt better, as though she were already on her way.

Back in the living room the fire had dwindled. Karyn put on another log and jostled the coals with the poker. New flames sprang up and crackled reassuringly.

"Karyn!"

The unexpected sound of her name startled her into dropping the poker. Someone, a man, had called from outside the house. Could it be Chris? But she had heard no car drive up.

She crossed quickly to the window. Roy's Ford was there, gleaming dully in the moonlight. That was all.

"Karyn!"

This time she recognized the voice. Roy. Calling her from somewhere outside. Why not at the door?

"Karyn!"

There was a throb of pain in the voice. Pain and something more.

From the edge of the window, standing close to the wall, she looked out to make sure the doorway was clear.

From the bookshelf, where Roy had left it, she took the flashlight. Holding it in one hand, she eased the door open just enough to look out.

"Roy, are you out there?"

"Help me, Karyn."

"Where are you? I can't see you."

"Over here. Come and help me."

Opening the door a little wider, Karyn swept the brush beyond the clearing with the beam from the flashlight. She moved the light along slowly until it picked out a face, pale against the shadows. Roy's face.

He was standing partially hidden by a clump of chapparal, looking at her. His expression was tortured. He seemed to strain toward her against invisible bonds.

Karyn stepped halfway through the doorway. "What is it, Roy? What's wrong?"

"Oh, Karyn." His voice was a strangled whisper.

He needed her, and for a moment everything else was forgotten. Karyn left the safety of the house and ran across the clearing toward her husband.

"No!" The single word was ripped from Roy's throat, then he vanished back into the shadows.

Karyn turned to run back to the house, then she froze. Standing between her and the door, its shoulders humped, the cruel mouth stretched into a canine grin, was the wolf. The beast's jaws opened and closed. It growled, a sound of unearthly evil.

Karyn could not get her breath. She stood paralyzed as the wolf came toward her stiff-legged, its eyes never leaving her face.

"Run, Karyn!"

The voice that shouted at her from somewhere back in the trees was like Roy's, and yet it was not like his. The sharp command freed her to move again. With the wolf between her and the house, Karyn turned to run in the other direction. Even as she broke away she felt the futility of trying to outrun the beast.

Abruptly the car was in front of her. Roy's Ford, only a few yards away. Karyn lunged the last few steps, jerked the door open, and fell inside. As she pulled the door closed behind her, the heavy body of the wolf thumped against the outside panel.

Karyn grasped the steering wheel and pulled herself upright. Through the window she saw the wolf up on its hind feet, paws braced against the car, biting at the door handle. Karyn punched the lock button down with her fist, then made sure the other doors were locked too. She slid to the far side of the seat and cowered there. The wolf, with its forepaws against the roof, glared in at her with a deeper hatred than Karyn would have believed possible on the face of a living creature.

A fogged patch grew and contracted on the window as the wolf breathed against the glass. Karyn could not pull her eyes away from its face. She pressed herself back against the far door.

Abruptly the wolf's head dropped out of sight. Karyn heard the rhythmic pad of its feet trotting away. Was it leaving? Karyn held her breath, not daring to hope.

There was silence for a moment, then a soft galloping sound and a jarring thud as the animal hit the side of the car. The Ford rocked with the impact. Karyn pulled herself up in the seat and saw the wolf gather itself and walk back to charge again. It turned ten yards away, crouched, and sprang forward like a greyhound after a rabbit. Six feet from the car the wolf leaped into the air and hit the door again with stunning force.

A spiderweb of cracks appeared on the window next to the driver's seat, and flecks of glass sprinkled the seat. In the fragmented view through the cracked window Karyn saw the wolf pick itself up and move away for another run. She knew there was no way to keep it out, and wondered if this was how Inez Polk had met her death.

A third time the wolf smashed into the side of the Ford. The damaged window shuddered and big chunks of glass fell away from the plastic core. It could not withstand many more blows.

Karyn jabbed a hand into her pocket, and her fingers closed around the leather case that held the car keys. She brushed the glass fragments from the seat and moved over behind the wheel, stabbing the key at the ignition lock on the side of the steering post.

Thump!

More glass sprayed across the inside of the car, and the plastic window core bulged inward. Karyn saw that her arm was bleeding, but paid no attention.

She found the ignition lock and twisted the key. The starter ground, the engine coughed and finally came to life. While she deliberately did not look at the wolf, Karyn struggled to remember the motions Roy went through in driving the car. She pressed down on the accelerator pedal and yanked the shift lever from *P* to *R*. The car lurched backward across the roadway and rammed into the brush on the far side. She knocked the shift lever back to *P* and fought to control her shaking hands.

She groped for the headlight switch, but could not find it. Outside in the moonlight she could see the wolf moving toward her. Forgetting the headlights, she cranked the steering wheel around to head toward town, stamped down on the accelerator, and forced the shift lever through the detents until the car jolted forward. The wolf sprang out of the way and vanished in the shadows as Karyn fought the wheel, fishtailing the car from one side of the narrow road to the other.

With only the moonlight to guide her, Karyn could barely make out the road. Tree branches slashed against the windshield as she veered from left to right and back again. She kept her foot heavy on the accelerator and battled to keep from plowing into the trees.

Without warning she hit the blacktop road that led into Drago. Traveling too fast to make the corner, Karyn stamped on the brake, but too late. With tires screaming, the Ford slid across the road and dived crazily into a drainage ditch on the far side.

The engine died. Karyn started to reach for the ignition key, but she saw by the steep angle of the car that it would be futile to try to drive out. She clawed open the door. The rest of the window fell out.

The cold wind whipped her hair into a tangle as she struggled up the side of the ditch onto the road. She looked up the lane toward the house, but saw nothing coming after her. Yet.

She started off at a run toward the village. She did not look back.

No light showed in the dreary buildings of Drago. The streets were deserted. Karyn crossed the short street where Dr. Volkmann lived. His house was dark, like the others. The Buick was not in the driveway. No sanctuary there.

On down the street she ran. The only sounds were the wind and the slap of her shoes on the pavement. Panic controlled her. She had no destination, she only knew that somewhere behind her *it* was coming.

Then there was a light. A blessed light up ahead in the store building. Safety. When she reached the door Karyn was sobbing with relief. She beat against the panel with the flat of her hand.

Oriole Jolivet opened up and peered through the doorway, her face a round caricature of surprise. "Karyn, what in the world are you doing here?"

"Let me in," Karyn gasped. The breath tore at her lungs. Her side hurt like a knife wound from running.

Oriole put an arm around Karyn and supported her as they walked back to the rear of the store. There was the light Karyn had seen from the street.

"Don't try to talk now, honey," Oriole said. "Just sit

yourself down here until you get your wind back."

Karyn sank gratefully into the wooden chair and let her head sink forward. Oriole stood by stroking her hair and making little clucking sounds of sympathy.

After many minutes Karyn's breathing slowed, though the pulse still pounded in her ears. "Thank God you were here, Oriole," she said.

"Sure, I'm here, honey." Oriole patted her shoulder awkwardly. "What happened to you?"

"Give me a little time, okay? I'm not quite ready to talk about it."

"Hey, I understand. How about a nice cup of hot coffee to perk you up?"

"I'd like that."

As Oriole went in back, slowly Karyn's nerves began to unknot. Her mind was still not ready to think about what had happened, but her body was beginning to relax.

Oriole returned with a mug of steaming coffee. "There you go. Don't drink it too fast, it's real hot."

As Karyn reached for the cup, Oriole saw the cut on her arm.

"Oh, look at that, you hurt yourself."

"It was glass. From the car window."

"You smashed up your car?"

Karyn nodded.

"You poor kid, no wonder you're shook up. Let me get something to put on that arm."

Oriole walked around behind Karyn's chair and rummaged in a cupboard. "There should be iodine in here, and I'll get bandages out of the stock up front."

The muffled sound of Oriole's last words made Karyn turn around in her chair. To her surprise, Oriole was pulling her sweater off over her head. She wore nothing underneath.

"What are you doing?" Karyn said.

Then Oriole pulled the sweater free, and Karyn saw

what was happening to the woman's face. Oriole smiled, and the blackened lips pulled back over a double row of sharp yellow teeth.

CHAPTER TWENTY-SEVEN

~~~~~~

Karyn sat stunned as Oriole Jolivet, or the thing that had been Oriole, continued to peel off clothing. Oriole's mouth and nose had pushed forward into a muzzle, and her skin was now covered with a coarse reddish hair. Acting by instinct rather than will, Karyn leaped to her feet and threw the cup of steaming coffee into the creature's face. Hearing a howl of pain, she ran out through the store to the front door.

Once she was outside Karyn stopped. She turned one way, then the other. Where could she go? Was there safety anywhere in this terrible night? With tears dimming her vision, Karyn began to run up the street. The darkened buildings of Drago seemed to crowd in on her from both sides.

Something was coming.

Karyn stopped and wiped her eyes. Moving silently

toward her down the middle of the street, eyes glittering in the moonlight, came a wolf.

"Oh, God, another one," Karyn cried. She turned back in the direction she had come from and was almost run down as a car slammed to a stop inches away from her.

Karyn dropped to her knees sobbing. The door of the old Buick opened and Dr. Volkmann jumped out. He ran around to the front of the car.

"Mrs. Beatty, what is it? What's wrong?"

She clutched at the doctor's coat and pulled herself erect. "Dr. Volkmann . . . help me . . . the wolves . . ."

Volkmann put an arm around Karyn and helped her into the car. He got in himself and sat behind the wheel with the engine idling. He watched Karyn carefully as she fought for composure.

"Oriole," she got out at last. "While I was with her just now she . . . changed."

"Are you saying Oriole Jolivet is a werewolf?" Volkmann's voice was calm and reassuring.

"Yes. And she's not the only one."

Something banged against the car, and for an instant the savage face of a wolf appeared at the window behind Volkmann. Karyn jerked away, but on her own side there was another, and more coming now from the dark buildings. One of them hit her window with its paws. Karyn ducked away and the side of her head cracked into the steering wheel. There was a flash of pain, and everything slipped out of focus.

Karyn's next sensation was one of floating. She was riding along on a gently flowing river. But there was danger. She had to swim to shore. She tried to move, but something held her fast. Suddenly awake, she thrashed wildly to free her arms and legs.

"It's all right." The voice of Dr. Volkmann was deep and commanding. "You're home now."

She was being carried, Karyn now saw, in Volkmann's arms. He was walking toward the little house, where the lights still blazed as she had left them.

"No!" she cried. "They're here too. The wolves."

Volkmann stopped and swung her feet down to the ground. He steadied her as she tried to stand. Her head hurt and she staggered against him.

"You say they're here?" Volkmann said.

"Yes. One came at me, but I got away in the car. I went into a ditch, then ran into town looking for some place to be safe. I found Oriole, and she . . ." Karyn could not complete the sentence. "We've got to get away."

The two of them turned back and started toward the Buick. Before they could get close, a lean black wolf slipped out of the forest and moved between them and the car. The wolf was joined by a second. Then a third.

"We'll never make it," Volkmann said. He spun Karyn back toward the house and they ran across the clearing to the door. Volkmann pushed it open and they stumbled inside. He slammed the door behind them and Karyn shot the bolt into place.

They stood for a moment watching the door as though expecting it to burst open.

"What about the back door and the windows?" Volkmann said.

"I locked everything before."

"Where is your husband?"

There it was, the thing Karyn had refused to think about. Part of her must have known when she found Roy's shoe near the place where Inez had died, but she would not let herself admit it. When he called her out of the house, she had gone, and *they* were waiting for her. She had lost him.

She said, "I think Roy is one of them."

Volkmann frowned and shook his head.

"I don't know how it could have happened," Karyn said.

"It must have been the night he did not come home,"

said Volkmann. "If he was attacked by a werewolf and lived . . ."

"But he had no wounds."

"None that showed, but remember the blood on his shirt."

Karyn turned away. She was not ready to talk about Roy. She went into the kitchen and ran a glass of cold water. Through the small window over the sink she saw more wolves coming out of the shadows.

"They're all around us," she said.

"We'll be safe inside the house."

"They broke the window of the car. They can get in."

Volkmann looked over to where the shotgun was propped against the wall.

Following his eyes, Karyn said, "That can't stop them."

"Perhaps it will slow them down."

"Can we make a run for the car?"

Volkmann peered out the front window, then turned back, his face grim. "Take a look."

Karyn moved closer to the window. What she saw froze her blood. The grassy clearing in front of the house was alive with wolves. Different shapes and shades, but all of them large and deadly-looking. Occasionally one of them or another would make a menacing move toward the house, but mostly they just shifted restlessly about, watching the house. Waiting.

Karyn backed away from the window, hugging herself for warmth. She spoke in a toneless voice, barely above a whisper. "Oh, the time we wasted wondering who in Drago was the werewolf. It isn't just one of them, it's the whole town. Inez must have realized that somehow. She was coming to warn me when they got her."

Volkmann continued to stare at the animals outside.

"It's the legend of Dradja," Karyn said. "The people would not give up their werewolf even under torture because the werewolf was all of them. When the village was destroyed some of them escaped. These things outside are their children."

"Incredible," Dr. Volkmann muttered.

"You've lived in Drago for years," Karyn said. "Did you never suspect?"

The doctor spoke without turning from the window. "I'm afraid I kept apart from the people of the town. Who could imagine a thing like this?"

Outside, the night sounds changed. Under the sighing of the wind there was a growing rustle of movement. A series of heavy blows thudded against the door, rattling dishes in the kitchen cupboards. A wolf crashed against one of the window screens and rebounded. Another hit a window on the opposite side.

Karyn and Dr. Volkmann looked at each other.

She said quietly, "They're coming for us."

The red Camaro hit the crest of the hill to the west of Drago and plunged down the winding road into the dark valley. At the wheel a grim Chris Halloran fought to keep the car on the road without slackening his speed. The gun loaded with silver bullets hung heavy but reassuring in his jacket pocket.

At last he reached the valley floor and the road straightened for the short drive to the village. As he entered Drago, Chris wondered why there were no lights. He slowed the car passing the dark buildings, looking for signs of life. He saw no one. Then what appeared to be a large dog showed up in the headlights. Chris hit the brake pedal and the car slewed to a stop. The animal never flinched, just stood there looking at him.

Now he saw it was not a dog. It was too big, and the eyes were not right. A wolf.

He started to ease the car around the animal, and a movement at the side of the street caught his eye. Another wolf was coming toward him. No, there were two of them. With a growing sense of alarm Chris looked along the street and saw half a dozen more of the shadowy forms. These were no common wolves.

He gunned the engine and wheeled the Camaro straight at the wolf that stood ahead of him. He tensed for the coming impact, but at the last instant the wolf sprang aside and the car roared past.

When he reached the turnoff to Karyn's house, Chris saw the rear end of a car jutting up from a drainage ditch across the road. He steered in that direction to let his headlights fall on the ditched car. A Ford. Roy Beatty's Ford.

Chris pulled the Camaro off on the shoulder and started to get out. He had one foot on the ground when a snarling beast charged him from the ditch. He pushed himself back inside and slammed the door just as the wolf hit the car.

His first thought was the gun. He drew the pistol from his pocket, then hesitated. He still had to reach Karyn. He could see there was no one in the Ford, so she must be at the house. He had only the twelve bullets, and from what he had seen so far he might need all of them.

Inside the house Karyn stood with her back to the inner wall next to the fireplace. She held the shotgun leveled at the door, in which two vertical cracks had opened under the constant battering from outside. She knew the gun was no defense, but it was better than waiting passively for . . . whatever.

On the other side of the fireplace, Dr. Volkmann stood watching intently as the cracks in the door widened with each blow. He had not spoken for several minutes. Nor had Karyn. There was nothing to be said.

Then, over the banging at the door and the rush of the wind, Karyn heard a new sound. The high-pitched whine of a straining engine. A car was coming. Coming fast. With a cry she dropped the gun and ran to the window. Bright white headlights washed across the clearing and the wolves.

"It's Chris!" she cried. "Dr. Volkmann, it's my friend. He'll help us."

Outside the Camaro plowed into the wolves, scattering them for a moment, and jolted to a stop behind the Buick.

"Dr. Volkmann, did you hear me? We're going to be all right."

Karyn turned to where the doctor was standing, but he was no longer there. His clothes lay on the floor. She started for the fallen shotgun, but a lean gray wolf sprang from the side of the room and stood between her and the weapon.

"Oh my God," Karyn gasped. "You too."

The wolf came at her.

CHAPTER TWENTY-EIGHT

The pack of ravening wolves around Karyn's house was like a preview of hell. Chris Halloran aimed the Camaro at two of the animals nearest the roadway and drove into them. He felt the sick-soft thump as the wolves went down under the wheels. They should have been crushed. Looking back, Chris saw the two animals lie still for a moment, then get back to their feet in jerky movements. Their eyes blazed with wild hatred.

Now he knew for certain what they were. His rational twentieth-century mind had rejected the word, but it had been on the edge of his consciousness from the time he had played the tape and heard Karyn ask for silver bullets. Werewolves.

He pulled up behind an old Buick that blocked his path to the house. Someone appeared for a moment at one of the windows. It might have been Karyn. Chris calculated his chances of reaching the house on foot. Between him and the door were more wolves than he could count. Right now they seemed indecisive, their attention divided between him and the house.

Chris took the gun from his pocket and stepped out of the car. The wolves watched him intently, but made no move. He started walking carefully toward the house. At the same time from inside came a loud growl. As though it were some kind of signal, the wolves came for him.

Chris took quick aim with the pistol and fired at the nearest animal. The sound was a disappointing little pop, and Chris longed for a heavier-caliber weapon. A puff of dust kicked up a foot in front of the wolf. He had missed. At pointblank range. One precious bullet gone.

For his second shot Chris steadied his right hand with his left, the way pistol shooting was taught. He aimed carefully at a point between the eyes and fired. A round black hole appeared magically in the short fur of the wolf's head. The animal's legs stiffened for a moment, then buckled, and it fell, the eyes open and empty.

The other wolves drew back for a moment, then came together in a mass between Chris and the door. Holding the gun straight out in front of him, he advanced cautiously. Off to one side, a lone pale wolf bounded from the forest and charged the house. Oblivious to both the man and the other animals, it crossed the clearing in powerful leaps and sprang for the window, forepaws outstretched to take the impact. The screen collapsed inward, the window glass shattered, and the pale wolf disappeared into the house. A woman screamed.

When she realized what had happened to Dr. Volkmann, Karyn edged away from the window, keeping her eyes on the lean gray wolf that now stood in her living room. She wanted to believe that Chris would reach her in time, but she had seen how many wolves blocked his approach to the house.

The muscles of the gray wolf bunched as he crouched to spring. With nowhere to go, Karyn backed into a corner, holding her arms crossed in front of her in a feeble attempt to ward off the attack.

But before the blow came there was a splintering crash and fragments of glass peppered the room. A pale-yellow wolf, broad through the chest, landed on all four feet between Karyn and the attacker. She screamed.

To Karyn's astonishment, the pale wolf turned not toward her, but the other way to face the lean Volkmann wolf. The two squared off, growling deep in their throats. The pale wolf made the first move, springing at the other. The gray wolf stepped nimbly aside, and the newcomer overshot and slammed into the sofa before he could turn. The gray wolf moved in fast, his jaws open wide, teeth bared for battle. They collided with a thump and rolled across the floor, the fury of their combat shaking the house. From outside Karyn heard the popping of a small-caliber gun.

She watched the fight with a strange detached fascination. The lean gray wolf was the quicker of the two, but the pale newcomer was the stronger. The gray wolf would back away, inviting an attack, then leap aside like a matador and slash at the other as he went by. Each time the sharp teeth ripped through the yellow fur, leaving a streak of blood, and each charge by the pale wolf was a fraction slower than the last.

The end came with startling suddenness. The gray wolf moved half a second too late, and the other was upon him. Using his superior weight, the pale wolf forced his foe slowly to the floor. Then he struck, powerful teeth clamping on the other's throat. A terrible, bubbling cry came from the downed animal just before his windpipe collapsed.

Still pressed back into the corner, Karyn looked directly into the eyes of the pale wolf as it raised its head, muzzle dripping with the other's blood. A shock of recognition went through her.

"Roy," she said softly.

At that moment the weakened door splintered and Chris Halloran burst into the room. He looked down at the mutilated wolf, then at the other. He pointed the Stoeger pistol at the survivor.

"No!" Karyn cried.

With his finger tight on the trigger, Chris looked over at Karyn.

"Don't kill him," she said. "Not this one."

Chris let his gun arm fall, and the pale wolf leaped out through the smashed window.

Karyn staggered for a moment, and Chris moved swiftly to catch her.

"Hang on," he said. "We've still got to get out of here."

She nodded and drew a shuddering breath. "How many bullets do you have left?"

"Only four, if I counted right."

Through the open doorway they could see the dark shapes moving cautiously nearer.

"We can't stay here," Karyn said. "We've got to get to the car."

Chris nodded toward the shotgun that lay across the room. "Can we use that?"

"It's no good. Only silver can stop them."

Outside the wolves grew bolder.

"Is there nothing else?" Chris asked.

"One thing," she remembered. "Fire."

Chris looked over at the dwindling flame in the fireplace. "See if you can find something to use for a torch. I'll watch the doorway."

Karyn ran to the bathroom and took Roy's long-handled shower brush from its hook over the tub. She wrapped two heavy towels around the bristle end, fastening them with adhesive tape. From the cupboard under the sink she took a can of lighter fluid and poured it over the towels. From out in the living room came the sound of shots. She ran back and saw two more wolves down on the floor.

Chris took the makeshift torch from her hand and touched the wrapped end to the fire. Flames enveloped the towels immediately.

"Stay close to me," he said, and led her out the front door.

Wolves were everywhere. They backed away when Chris thrust the torch at them, but just far enough to avoid the flame. He fired at one and killed it.

As they inched across the clearing the wolves circled them like a city gang of juveniles waiting for an opening to attack.

Chris handed her the gun. "You take this. I'll try to scatter them with the torch while you make for the car. There's one bullet left. If you have to use it, make it count."

"What about you?"

"Once you're inside the car, be ready to whip the door open for me. When I come, I'll come fast."

Karyn squeezed his arm, then gripped the pistol firmly and started running. She forced herself to look nowhere but straight ahead at the car. With every step she expected to be pulled down from behind by powerful jaws. Behind her she could hear the frenzied growling of the wolves as Chris menaced them with the torch.

The blood pounded in Karyn's temples as she covered the last yards to the car. Just two steps away from safety a lithe black wolf sprang between her and the car. For a frozen moment the woman and the beast were face to face. The green eyes of the wolf blazed with hatred. The timeless hatred of the female.

"I should have known it was you, Marcia," said Karyn.

The she-wolf gathered herself and leaped at her. At the same instant Karyn fired. One of the green eyes burst like a ripened grape as the bullet pierced it and sank into the brain. The black wolf screamed once and tumbled life-less to the ground at Karyn's feet.

She stepped over the animal's body and snatched open the door on the passenger's side of the Camaro. Without looking back she dived inside and slammed the door be-hind her.

As Karyn pulled herself upright she saw Chris running toward the car with the torch held out in front of him. He slammed into the fender, did a body roll across the hood, and came down on the driver's side still gripping the torch. Karyn banged the door open for him, and he levered him-self inside, hurling the torch back at the raging wolves.

The burning torch traced a fiery spiral arc through the night and landed in the dry grass. The wind caught the flame, and in seconds it had spread across the clearing to the oily chaparral at the edge of the forest.

Chris got the car going, swung around, and sped back toward the road leading out. Behind them they could hear the growing roar of flames and screams that were neither animal nor human.

They did not slow down until they reached the crest of the mountain. There Chris pulled to a stop and they looked back. Below them in the valley the red-orange glow of the fire had spread into the village of Drago, whipped on by the desert wind.

"Some of them will get away," Karyn said.

Chris did not answer.

She looked down at the fire as it ate through the wooden buildings and thought of the long-dead village of Dradja. "Some of them always get away."

A sudden deep chill made her shudder. Chris put an arm around her shoulder and drew her close to him. In a little while the chill subsided.

"Can we go away from here?" she said. "Far away?"

"Yes," he said. He pulled the car back onto the road and drove on over the mountain.

Just as they started down the other side Karyn heard it. She clapped her hands over her ears, but could not shut it out. The howling.

GREAT ADVENTURES IN READING